NECRO

"Magic is just a tool. It's what you do with it that determines whether it's evil or not."

Lord Timikia

By C.W. Suttle

Published by Suttle Enterprises, LLC
Novi, Michigan

Cover Art by Oscar Salcedo (A.K.A. Ooki)
https://www.artstation.com/ooki
Cover titles and layout by C.W.Suttle

Edited by Joyous Seeman
www.linkedin.com/in/joyous-seeman-902a8422

ISBN: 979-8-9860148-0-7

Discover more about the World of the Necro at

www.necro-world.com

Character Name Pronunciations
World Maps
Author Commentary
Tee Shirts and other Collectables
AND MORE!!

Chapter #1

The Test

Her quill danced over a mound of pages. The pressing burdens of leadership lay heavy upon her brow. Though hints of gray wound through her long blond locks, she retained a youthful gleam in her eye. Was I the only one that sensed the sadness in her soul?

At last, the quill paused. With a deep sigh, she prepared herself for the next difficult task. I was never quite sure why I spied on her; perhaps, I was hoping a piece of her strength would rub off on me.

"TIMIKIA! How many times have I told you not to do that?"

I smirked a boyish grin. "Sorry, Mother. I hate to disturb you … but it's time."

"Are you ready?" Queen Lika gazed at me with a mother's love and a nursemaid's concern.

"As ready as I will ever be," I said, my lip quivering as the gravity of the moment crashed down upon me.

"Are you scared?"

"Y-y-yes." My gaze dropped to the floor. I felt a tear welling up in my eye that I fought to contain.

"Your father would have been proud of you. Lord Whispa too."

"What if I can't do it? What if … if I … if I can't pass the test?"

"You will," Mother comforted. "Even if you don't, you are still Prince Timikia heir to the throne."

"That's not enough! I'm the son of Lord Timicus, God Emperor of the Dead. What if I disgrace his name? What if I disgrace Lord Whispa? What if I disgrace you … or myself?"

"What did Lord Whispa always tell you?"

"Believe in me. Believe in the magic within me. My father lives on through me," I answered.

Mother's smile curled up from the side of her lip. "Lord Whispa was a wise man, a wonderful mentor, and a good judge of talent. He believed in you. You must believe in yourself. This sun, more than ever."

I nodded as the quiver returned to my lips. For moons, the burden of the test had been growing in the deepest regions of my soul, making sleep difficult and my appetite had all but disappeared. I felt a dull throbbing at the base of my neck as Mother stood up and approached me. She reached down and gently kissed my forehead. The glistening gaze of her crystal blue eyes calmed me. I could feel my power and pride returning.

Taking my hand, we walked down the long Hallway of the Honored Dead. As I passed each massive painting of the great necromancer lords, it felt like I had known them personally. Countless times I walked these halls with Lord Whispa. I listened intently as he rambled on with every story and myth of each lord in mind-numbing detail. But the last picture on the right, I knew better than all the rest combined—the picture of Lord Timicus, God Emperor of the Dead, my father. The picture was so life-like it almost spoke to me. Since I had never heard my father's voice, I wondered if my imagination was correct, but somehow it was comforting none the less. When I reached the massive painting, I stopped to have one more silent conversation with him.

"I can feel his strength in you," Mother said, while stroking my head.

"For so many winters, Lord Whispa had been preparing me for this sun. I never thought too much about the test. The twelfth anniversary of my birth seemed so far away. Now it's here, just like the test."

"I imagine your father is watching you from the other side right now. You're going to do fine."

"How do you live up to the shadow of a god?"

"Your father was not a god, just a man. God Emperor of the Dead is just a given title."

"Lord Whispa always told me that too. But his painting is still in the honored hall … in a sacred place, watching and judging every pledge that attempts the test of Nocmara." I took a final gaze at the powerful image of my father, then turned toward the giant brass doors of Nocmara Hall. Two guards garbed in black armor opened the doors as I approached. Before we could pass the threshold, we were stopped.

"I'm sorry, Lika," the guard said, raising his hand to block the

Queen's path. "This is as far as you can go."

"I am Queen Lika. You WILL let me pass!" said Mother, surprised and annoyed.

"In this place, you are neither Queen nor Lady. Within the walls of Nocmara, you are only Lika. You know this. Due to your kinship to the late Lord Timicus, you have been allowed to come this far. If you wish, you may watch the proceeding from the upper balcony in silence."

Mother nodded with a scowl. Outside these walls, she was a powerful monarch, but she knew the law. She looked down at me and mustered a comforting smile. Leaving me with the ominous guards, she proceeded up the steps.

I entered the chamber where three boys were sitting on a long wooden bench. I approached and sat next to the short one, who seemed small for twelve. He was meticulously clothed in a fine red and gold dress, the markings of a rich family. But, as fine as his clothes were, the look on his face told me all I needed to know. He was frightened too.

"Hello, I'm Prince Timikia."

"Not here you're not," spat a tough-looking kid at the far end of the bench. "Here, you're just Timikia. We're all the same here. Just pledges to the Brotherhood. The test will prove who has the real stuff. Sleeping on fancy pillows doesn't make you a necromancer."

"Timikia?" questioned the short boy. "Aren't you the son of Lord Timicus?"

I gave a quick nod, not wanting to boast.

"Oh, you're going to pass for sure."

"Don't count on it," interrupted the tough one. "I, Paraton, will be the one they take. I will be the one they pick. Look at my hand."

He thrust his open palm in front of our faces. It was scarred and blackened.

"I have been burning my hand every sun for moons to get ready to hold the wand. I can't fail. Remember that name, Paraton, for a sun will come when you will bow to it." Paraton pulled his hand back in triumph and marched off to sit alone.

"Would burning your hand help?" whispered the short boy, cupping his hand over his mouth.

"No," I replied, quite sure of myself.

"My name is Emerus," the boy said. "What a time to choose to take the test. I have to compete against you?"

"Despite what Para—whatever his name is—believes, we are not in competition. Anyone who can hold the wand is moving on."

"My father told me that sons of great lords almost always become necromancers."

"Not always. Many are too afraid to even try and many others fail," I said.

"I'm from the Kingdom of Pillico," Emerus began. "My mother almost made it to the fourth rank of the Order of the Druids."

My eyebrows raised. "Druids? And they are still letting you take the test? Aren't they afraid you might be a spy?"

"My mother died at the Battle of Versonic, fighting alongside the necromancers. She gave her life to save a lord. They all said she was a hero. I never really knew her."

"I'm sorry." My brow deepened for I knew his pain.

The door to the chambers creaked open and an older necromancer lord walked in. His powerful presence filled the room. He was cloaked in a dark cape draped to the floor. One side slung over his belt to show off an impressive wand. A large demon's skull adorned the silver staff. The skull was blackened from use in battle.

In a deep voice, he inquired, "Who wants to be first?"

"I'll be first," cried Paraton, leaping up from his seat. Filled with pride and arrogance, he marched off to the judging room. He stopped at the door, turned his head, and smirked at the rest of us. The guards closed the door, leaving me and the others alone with our thoughts. Emerus rushed to the door in an attempt to listen.

"I can't hear anything. Dang, I want to know what's going on."

"What difference does it make?" said the third boy, who had been silent up till now. "If he makes it, we'll probably never see him again. If he doesn't, we'll know soon enough."

"How will we know?" Emerus asked.

An ear-piercing scream ripped through the brass doors and filled the chamber with horror. Gasps of agony and cries for mercy chilled our bones. Shrieks of pain were followed by low whimpers. Emerus slowly backed away from the door his face as white as bleached bones.

"He failed," added the silent one into the dreaded stillness of the room.

The doors swung open. Two guards were dragging the nearly lifeless body of Paraton from the judging room. The only sign of life was the constant twitching of his arm. Emerus looked like he was going to throw up as they dragged Paraton off like useless trash.

The older necromancer entered the room and in the same low voice uttered, "Who's next?"

We were all silent, barely breathing.

"How about you, Timikia?"

I nodded with trepidation. The lord motioned me into the judging room. It was not what I expected. I had always envisioned a magnificent chamber with tall benches for the judging lords to look down from on high. Instead, it was a small, dark room, lit by tiny candles. The judging lords were sitting at a table, their faces darkened by the dim light.

"At last," commented one of the lords with his face shrouded in a hood, "the great Timikia. We have been waiting for your twelfth anniversary for a long time. I pray you do better than the last pledge."

The lord reached out, placing a small box on the table in front of me. I dreaded what I knew I had to do. I opened the box and there it was—the testing wand. The head of a small odd bird on the pommel of an old, withered stick. It didn't look like much, but wands often don't.

"All I have to do is hold it," I said to myself again and again. I reached for the wand but paused with it just outside of my grasp. Praying the judges wouldn't notice, I tried to still my quivering fingers. All my life I had prepared for this one moment and still I had no idea what to expect. I closed my eyes, gathered my courage, and grabbed the wand.

Searing pain shot up my arm, across my shoulders, and down my spine. It felt like a thousand spiders were digging their fangs into my body. I gritted my teeth and grimaced. In the dark, hidden balcony, I knew my mother was suffering right along with me.

Fighting back against the pain, I slowed my breathing and unclenched my teeth. With each passing moment, I could feel pride growing in my chest knowing that I was going to pass the test. I looked into the eyes of the five judges with confidence.

After I had stared down the last lord, the chief judge said, "Impressive, you may put down the wand."

I dropped the wand into the box as fast as my fingers would open. The pain began to subside, except for the burning in my fingertips. My palm was bright red as if had been scalded by hot oil.

"Impressive indeed. I, Lord Mar, vote to accept Timikia into training at Nocmara."

"I, Lord Kopla, also vote in favor of Timikia."

"Big DEAL! It's a training wand," spat the lord draped in purple. "Any bum off the street could hold that. Let's see him hold this."

He retrieved an ornate, gold-inlaid box from his cloak and placed it on the table. He lifted the lid.

"Lord Timicus's wand," said Lord Mar. "How did you get that? It is supposed to be locked away."

"What difference does it make? The question still stands. Can the boy hold THIS wand?"

"You don't have to do this, Timikia," Lord Kopla declared. "Your demonstration was more than good enough to pass. You don't need Lord Loter's vote."

"Of course," snickered Lord Loter, "majority rules. He doesn't need my vote. He can walk away from my challenge. Afterall—isn't that what a sniveling little dog does?"

"DON'T DO IT!" cried my mother from the balcony.

"Silence, WOMAN!" Lord Loter screamed. "Or I will not only remove you from the balcony but from the entire school."

Lord Loter glared into the darkness of the balcony before turning his attention back to me.

"Can you believe she did that? What else would you expect of a peasant?" Lord Loter snickered.

"SHE IS NOT A PEASANT!" My voice reverberated through the rafters.

"Watch yourself, boy. I'll give you that one because of who you are, but if you ever raise your voice to me again, I will kill you. I'll stomp you out like a little bug. Your father was the son of a miller. Your mother nothing more than a scullery maid. Face it, son, you're the bastard child of a whore."

"THAT'S ENOUGH, LORD LOTER," Lord Mar barked.

"I don't think so," Lord Loter sneered. "You know the rules. I get to say or do anything I want before I vote."

"I am Timikia, son of Lord Timicus, God Emperor of the Dead."

Lord Loter emitted a raucous laugh. "You are no Lord Timicus. Your father could have grabbed this wand and held it all sun. I'll vote for you, boy, but I want everyone here to see that you are no Lord Timicus. Your bloodline has been washed out. Poisoned by a peasant's urine in the water."

"MY MOTHER IS NOT A PEASANT!" I balled up my fists.

"THEN PROVE IT! GRAB THE WAND!"

I snatched the wand from the box. What came next, I only know what my mother told me. I screamed like a banshee from hell. I fell on my butt, quivering like a leaf in a storm. I foamed at the mouth. My mother leapt over the railing, a ten-foot drop to the floor, and ran to help me, but she was restrained by the guards. It was at this time I began to regain consciousness. The top of my head felt like it was being ripped off by boney claws. My bones felt like they were exploding from the inside. I could hear my mother fighting with the guards and Lord Loter laughing with delight.

And then it quieted. Wispy forms started filling the room. I could see through them as if they were smoke. They were everywhere. The wisps swirled in a dance of darkness around me. One passed right through my body, sending a cool chill up my spine. Fear was becoming greater than my pain.

"He sees," Lord Mar said with a look of awe on his face.

"That's impossible!" Lord Loter argued. "No pledge sees. I have graduated guardians that couldn't see yet."

"He sees," Lord Mar repeated. "Look at the fear in his eyes. Look at the anguish on his face. Nothing but the sight could cause that."

Lord Mar stood and dashed toward me. The blood had drained from my face. He yanked the wand from my clutches. The wisps vanished as I flopped over in a fetal position. Lord Mar stepped back to the table and returned the wand to its box. He shook his hand with a little wince as he put down the magic stick. I was still quivering in the corner.

"I, Lord Mar, vote to admit Timikia."

Lord Loter tightened his lips in anger. "I vote yes."

Chapter #2

In the Queen's Eye

I couldn't believe my eyes. Loter had always been a monster to me, but watching him terrorize my son was more than I could bear.

"DON'T DO IT!" I cried.

"Silence, WOMAN!" Loter screamed, "or I will not only remove you from the balcony but from the entire school."

Trembling with rage, I again balled up my fists. Two guards emerged from the shadows in silent warning.

Come on son, I thought, *don't let him get to you. You're better than him.*

Loter barraged Timikia with cruel insults. With his face flushing, Timikia snarled.

"THEN PROVE IT! GRAB THE WAND!" Loter barked.

My worst fears were coming true. Timikia grabbed my consort's wand. An unholy clamor exploded from his throat. Eyes rolling back in his head, he fell to the floor twitching with violent convulsions. As I rushed to the balcony's edge, a guard grabbed me. Turning, I kneed him hard. I leapt over the wall, crashing down to the stone floor below. Pain shot through my right ankle. I didn't let it stop me. I was desperate to free him from the grip of the wand. Before I could reach him, a guard grabbed my wrists. I struggled to free myself, but he was too strong. I head-butted him in the nose, still, he held fast. A second guard engulfed my waist, lifting my feet off the ground. Kicking and squirming I tried to bite them. I stopped cold when I heard …

"He sees."

"That's impossible," Loter argued, "no pledge sees. I have graduated guardians that couldn't see yet."

"He sees. Look at the fear in his eyes. Look at the anguish on his face. Nothing but the sight could cause that."

As I stood in stunned silence, the guards released me. Stepping up to Loter, I slapped him hard across his nasty little face. Blue emoting smoke streamed upward from his eyes. As he reached for his wand, Lord Mar interceded pushing me back a step. The two elder lords stared each other down.

"I, Lord Mar, vote to admit Timikia."

Loter's eyes returned to their normal, hateful black.

"I vote yes."

"You could have KILLED HIM," I spat.

Shooting me a vile look, Loter stomped out of the chambers.

"It is not wise to anger Lord Loter," Lord Mar said.

"It is not wise to anger Queen Lika," I retorted.

I limped to my son's side. Kneeling, I lifted his head onto my lap. His eyes were having trouble focusing. His lips trembled.

"Did I pass?"

Vomit covered his chin. The fingers of his right hand were still twitching. Blood was dripping from his fingernails.

"Just be quiet, my son. You need rest."

A huge tear rolled down my cheek and splashed onto the stone floor.

"Did I pass?"

"Yes. Yes, you passed."

With that, he fell limp in my arms. The lords and guards watched in silence until my tears subsided. Lord Mar took my hand and helped me to my feet. He had cold eyes, but a gentle voice.

"Come, Lika. It's time for you to leave."

"But I have to take care of my son!"

"You know what has to happen now. Timikia must advance to the training. You will not hear from him again for many winters."

"Promise me he won't die. Promise me."

"I will look after him personally. Hopefully, he will return to you a necromancer fledgling."

"Or a corpse."

Lord Mar motioned to the guards. They lifted Timikia by his arms, dragging him from the room. They disappeared through a mysterious black door, a door as black as my soul felt at that moment. I buried my head into my hands.

"What have I done? Why did I let him take this wretched test?"

"Because it's what he wanted. Your consort was a good friend. We both know what Lord Timicus went through to become a necromancer lord. This passion burns in Timikia's soul as well. It burns in all those wishing to become a lord. It's the only way to survive the trials. Worry will eat you alive. You're better off returning to your palace and pretending that Timikia was never born. It's the only way to maintain your sanity."

"I can't do that."

Lord Mar smirked, "Neither could my mother."

"Did he really see? Did he see the other side?"

"I believe he did. When he recovers from being stupid enough to grab Lord Timicus's wand, I will speak with him about his experience. Only then, can I be positive."

"Why don't necromancers ever talk about the other side? I had asked Lord Whispa many times to describe it to me. He would never speak of it."

"Because we can't, my Lady."

"Why? Is it some kind of necromancer law or code?"

"No, nothing like that. We can't because you would never understand. There is no way to put it into words you could comprehend."

"Try me. I'm pretty smart."

"Oh—that I know. Trust me. I've known you for many winters. Stupid is not a word I would used to describe you. It's not a matter of being smart. Imagine that you have never seen a color in your entire life. All you've ever seen is black, white, and gray. How would I explain the color blue to you? You would have no frame of reference on which you could draw. The only way to understand the other side—is to see it."

"I wish I could see it. Somewhere on the other side is my beloved Timicus. What I would do to see him one more time."

"You will, when it's your turn to cross. I'm sure Lord Timicus is patiently awaiting you."

I hobbled on my sprained ankle as Lord Mar escorted me from the chambers. To relieve the pain, he pulled a healing potion from his belt. I pulled the cork, releasing a horrid aroma. The taste was even worse. I gulped it down fast and still I gagged. With a tingle, much of the pain in my ankle evaporated.

"Thank you. I will send the one thousand gold to pay for it."

"No need. This one is on me. I fought alongside your consort in many a battle. Sometimes he'd toss me one so I could make it home. I owe you this one—and many more."

Outside, terror flashed in the eyes of the two remaining pledges, still awaiting their turn. I felt for them and their mothers who couldn't be here. Rank has its privileges. We walked down the Hall of the Honored Dead and back to the entrance of Nocmara. Loter was arguing with two other lords. As we approached, the others departed and Loter scowled at me.

"How dare you interrupt these proceedings? You're banned from this school for life."

"How dare you pull a stunt like that? And you're banned from my palace for life."

"No great loss," he spat and plodded down the hall.

Lord Mar frowned.

"You do like living dangerously."

"I've faced down worse since taking the throne."

"Lord Loter's abilities are not to be trifled with. As a member of the Council, he is a dangerous enemy."

"So am I."

With a smirk he bade me farewell. After the massive doors closed, I pressed my forehead against them.

"Take care, my son. Come back to me, even if it is just as a normal man. I love you so."

A single tear trickled down my face. My ladies-in-waiting came rushing to my side.

"Is everything all right, my Lady?" inquired Soronto, my most trusted confidant. "Did Prince Timikia pass the test?"

"Yes."

"That is terrific news!"

I looked back at the drab stone walls of Nocmara.

"I hope so ... I hope so."

Chapter #3

The Room

Everything hurt. I felt like I'd been dragged behind a chariot for suns. Even breathing was painful. Raising my head caused a gripping pain across my shoulders. From the corner of my aching eyes, a dark figure loomed next to the bed. If he meant me harm, there would be little I could have done to stop him. I struggled for a better view.

"L-L-Lord Mar," I said, stuttering in a low growl.

"Try to rest. You're suffering from the agonies. Powerful wands can do that. By the end of the sun, it should subside. Before you're taken away to the room, I need to know what you saw."

His question was unclear, but I knew exactly what he meant.

"I don't know. I can't describe it. They were there, but they weren't. Just things in the air. Did I imagine it all?"

"No, you saw the other side. It's never been done by someone your age before."

"How? Why?"

"Lord Loter thinks that your mother's peasant beginnings weakened your bloodline. I have known your mother many winters. There's a strength to her. The first time your father met her, he saw it too. That's why he chose her to be his consort. That's what he loved about her. Your mother didn't weaken your bloodline. She strengthened it. Being the son of Lord Timicus is a heavy burden. There are many expectations of you. There are some who want to see you fail and fail hard. Lord Timicus was the peasant turned God Emperor of the Dead. The only one ever. There are those who hated him for that and hence you. Rumors of you having the sight have spread across the school. That is not a good thing. It's best that a pledge keeps a low profile—quiet, and in the shadows. Being noticed breeds jealousy. There is no chance of you escaping scrutiny now. Your next trial is the room. What did Lord

Whispa tell you about the room?"

"What's the room?"

"Lord Whispa was a clever one. Be strong, boy."

He left without so much as a goodbye. Sitting up caused searing pain behind my eyes. Lying down didn't help much either. The angle of the light let me know it was about half-sun. I finally managed to sit up. There I sat as the sun continued across the sky.

As dusk approached, I could stand, as predicted by Lord Mar. The pounding in my head eased. I heard high-pitched clicks of footsteps on the stone floor grow louder. They were the heavy metal-toed boots of soldiers or perhaps guards. Two burly men and a cleric entered the room. The cleric's light footsteps were soundless as he approached and removed his hood. The lines on his face made him appear a hundred winters old. Wrinkles so deep, I thought they would bleed.

"Do you wish to quit?"

His voice was low, serious, and in monotone.

"No."

"You are not trapped here. You are not a prisoner. You can quit anytime, but if you do, you can never return. Do you understand?"

"I understand."

He held out a small, unassuming redwood box.

"This is your training wand. Protect it with your life. If you lose it or break it, you will be tossed out of Nocmara for good. Follow me."

The cleric walked in a peculiar manner. He seemed to float. We traversed down three hallways to a stairwell. The further we descended, the darker it grew, until only the guards' torches lit the way. Reaching the bottom, I was led to a small wooden door with strong iron hinges. The cleric turned to address me.

"This is the room. Once you enter, there are only three ways to leave. One is to quit. Two is to die. Three, hold your wand for five hundred breaths. The room is not a pleasant place. So, I will ask you again, do you wish to quit?"

"No."

The guards opened the door and a foul odor escaped. It was a repelling stench. Three other boys were sitting on the floor. They looked up, expressionless. The guards shoved me in and locked the door behind me. The room fell into complete darkness.

"What is this place?"

A very thin voice replied, "Hell."

I felt around for the wall and sat down on the floor.

"What … what am I supposed to do now?"

"Shut up and sleep."

Sleep? Like I was going to sleep. I explored my wand box discovering a small clasp. Carefully opening the box, my fingers probed around the edges. I should have waited for a source of light before attempting to examine the wand, but my curiosity was overwhelming.

"Ouch!"

It felt like needles pricking my fingertips.

"No practice at night! That's the rule. Go to sleep now!"

The boy's voice was stern and demanding. I closed the box and tucked it into my vest.

Why didn't Lord Whispa tell me about this place? This trial? He warned me about the test, but never mentioned the room. I tried to sleep, I even wanted to sleep, but my mind was whirling. Time crawled. It was the longest night of my life.

As dawn arrived, a dim light filtered in from a square hole in the ceiling. The sunlight grew brighter with each passing moment. The other shabbily dressed boys began to stir. One boy, pale and thin like the others, was banging his head against the wall. I tried to stop him. He just pulled away with a shrug and continued.

"Don't bother," said the oldest boy, his long black hair framing the despair on his face. "The kid is a goner. He won't make it much longer. Better to just let him go."

I sat next to him hoping to gain some insight into this stone purgatory in which I found myself.

"Hi, I'm Timikia," I said, flashing him a weak smile.

"I don't care. You'll just come and go like the rest of them."

"How many suns have you been here?"

"Suns? I don't know. I'd be more interested in how many winters I've been here."

"WINTERS!"

He smirked, "Yeah. I've been here longer than anyone. You'll be just like the rest—banging on the door to quit within a moon. I saw one kid die. I've only seen two conquer the room. Looking at the likes of you, I doubt you'll succeed either."

"Might I inquire how long you've held your wand?"

"At my best—a little over two hundred breaths. The training wand is more wicked than the test wand. You'll find that out soon enough. I still have a long way to go."

"What's your name?"

"Well—not that it matters. You probably won't be around long enough for us to become friends or anything like that. It's Tomus."

I was jolted from the conversation by the third boy heavily panting in the corner. He was holding his wand. Tomus starting counting in a whisper.

"Twenty-one, twenty-two, twenty-three …"

Grimacing in pain, the boy dropped the wand to the floor. He grabbed his wrist trying to stop the tremors.

"Less than last sun. Are you going to give it a try?" Tomus said.

I retrieved the box from my vest. Most wands have a twisted stem, mine was quite straight. The skull of a small lizard-like creature adorned the crown. It didn't look like much, but I knew from experience that looks can be deceiving. Within the first few breaths after picking up the wand, I was fighting through the pain. Tomus started counting.

"Thirteen, fourteen, fifteen …"

That was all I could take. After dropping the wand back into the box, I tried to ease the pain by opening and closing my fingers.

"Fifteen. Not bad for a first try. Don't try more than a few times a sun for a while. You don't want to lose the use of your arm. I've seen that happen before."

"When do they let us out to eat?"

"Let us out? They don't let us out for anything. Why do you think it smells so bad in here? The smell is not the room, it's us. You relieve yourself in that bucket in the corner. They pick it up once a sun when they bring in the food."

"Speaking of food, when is breakfast?"

Tomus smirked, "We get one meal a sun. Quiet now, I need to practice."

Tomus started warming up. He would pick up the wand for about thirty breaths and then rest for a bit. Each resting period he would massage the inside of his wrist and chant something under his breath. I wasn't sure if it was some type of spell or a positive message of encouragement. Through it all, he never spoke or looked up. This went on most of the morning.

A large wrap on the door broke Tomus's concentration. A small flap at the bottom of the door opened. Four bowls were slid into the room. The other two boys didn't move; they just stared at the bowls. The headbanger kept banging his head.

A low voice from the other side of the door inquired, "Does anyone want to quit?"

No one said a word. The flap on the door lowered and latched. Like ravenous dogs, the two boys ran for the bowls. I surveyed the contents of my bowl: a stale hunk of bread, a small carrot, and a tiny piece of grayish meat. Who knows what type of animal it came from?

"This is it for the entire sun?"

"Yeah. Get used to being hungry."

The headbanger stayed in the corner banging his head.

"What about him? What about his food."

"We can divide it up later. Shut up and eat."

I ate the meager meal. It was awful, but I was hungry. I worried about the headbanger the whole time. After picking up the fourth bowl, I stood up. Tomus grabbed my arm and stopped me in my tracks.

"I said we would divide the food later!"

"I'm going to try and feed him."

"Don't be stupid. He's done. He just doesn't know it yet. That food is better used by the three of us."

With a scowl, I yanked my arm free. Grabbing the headbanger by the shoulders, I pulled him away from the wall. He fought me, but he was emaciated and quite weak. I held the bread to his lips. He wrenched his head trying to avoid the nourishment as if it was poison. I didn't give up. Finally, he took a bite. That calmed him down. Bite by bite, I fed the poor, tormented boy. By the end, he was slumped in my arms staring at the floor. When he had finished, he looked up at me with a blank stare. I couldn't tell what he was thinking—if he was thinking anything at all.

"You think you're noble," Tomus said. "You're just wasting food."

Tomus began his main attempt for the sun, mouthing the numbers with each breath. Near the end, his face was twitching and contorting as he tried to hang on for a few more breaths. With a wince, he dropped the wand to the floor.

"Two hundred and fourteen. Is that good?" I asked.

"Two better than last sun. At my current rate, I may only be here another winter."

He went to the corner and sat in silence rubbing his wrist.

For the first time, I turned my attention to the quiet boy. He had not said a word all sun. I had been so intent on studying Tomus's techniques that I had barely noticed him.

"So, what's your story?" I asked, sitting down next to him.

He studied me for some time before replying.

"Story? It's more like a play of horrors. I've been here fifty-six suns and I'm only up to twenty-eight breaths. What's so great about being a necromancer anyway?"

"There is nothing more honorable than being a necromancer. They are the most powerful people in the entire Southern Realm, maybe in all of Atlantis. A necromancer lord is almost a god."

"Yeah, and it takes like forty-five winters to become one. Forty-five winters of this crap? I'll be insane by then."

"Forty-five winters from now, you'll be dead of old age. But as a necromancer, you can live multiples of that."

"Only if you survive the poisoning. Do you know how many necromancers die from the poisoning? I heard it's like one in three. Imagine putting up with all this crap for thirty winters just to die in agony at the hands of the green death."

"If you truly feel that way, why not quit?"

The boy looked sad. "My father wants this more than life itself. If I fail now, he will disown me. I have to at least make fledgling to stay in his good graces."

"My father is dead, but I sort of feel that way too. What do you say we work together? Share ideas. Cheer each other on. Anything would be better than being in a room with three total strangers."

His eyes were serious. After a few moments of consideration, he nodded. I patted him on the shoulder with a smile.

"It's almost dusk. I'm going to make one more attempt before dark. The name is Timikia."

"Pourous."

"I need to ask a question of you, Pourous. Why is it that we can't practice at night?"

"Because the screams wake everyone up."

Chapter #4

Worse

Sun six. It feels like I've been down here for a winter. Tomus was right about being hungry. Thoughts of my empty stomach dominated my suns. Despite improving faster than the others, I still had a long way to go. My best was forty-two breaths. I passed Pourous on my fourth sun. Trying not to discourage him, I chose to lie about my results. He was holding firm around twenty-eight or nine. Tomas and I spoke only when needed, but Pourous is more forthcoming. I've heard a lot of stories about his dad. They were not good.

"Good morning, Pourous. How did you sleep?"

"Ah … you know."

I didn't sleep well either. An odd occurrence had been troubling me all night. I was dying to tell Pourous about it.

"Last sun, I noticed something strange about my wand."

"Strange?"

"The lizard skull was moving during one of my attempts."

"Nah, you're just hungry," Pourous said. "This place will do that to you."

"I hope I'm not hallucinating after only six suns."

"You're fine. Don't think about it. How did you do last sun?"

"Twenty," I said, finding it difficult to make eye contact as I lied.

"WOW. Twenty … after only six suns. You're flying. It took me two moons to get there. Tomus told me you're the son of Lord Timicus. Is that true?"

"Yeah."

"Why didn't you tell me?"

"It was made clear to me when I arrived that here I'm just Timikia, the worthless pledge. Nothing more."

"Is it true that your father could steal the minions of other necromancers?"

"No. He could only release them back to the other side. That's why none of the other necromancers would dare challenge him. He could wipe out their forces with a single spell."

"Whoa."

Lord Whispa told me about my father's release spell. A spell that no other necromancer knew or understood. My father took the spell to his grave, wherever that may be. He feared a long and bloody war would be the result of sharing it. Some spells are too powerful for this world.

I glanced over at Banger, the nickname I adopted for our wall-pounding friend. He was eating now. It had been suns since he last bashed his head into the wall. In front of my eyes, his improved disposition shifted into a mix of sadness and pain. Before I could comfort him, he ran headfirst into the wall. The sound of his skull cracking against the rocks was horrifying. I hurried to his side as he collapsed on the floor. The gray wall was splattered in crimson. Pounding on the door, I screamed for help.

I heard slow steps coming down the hallway.

"HURRY!"

"What's with all the ruckus?" the guard asked through the door.

"There's been a serious injury. We need help, NOW!"

"Is he dead?"

"I don't know—maybe. He will be soon if you don't open this damn door."

The creaking latch turned. Stepping into the room, the guard saw Banger on the ground. He seemed in no rush to check on him.

"Wait here. Don't touch him."

The guard left. He returned with a necromancer guardian. The guardian knelt over Banger. After placing two fingers on his neck, he nodded to the guard.

"Get him out of here," the guardian ordered.

The guard dragged Banger from the room leaving a trail of blood.

"Wait a minute," I yelled. "That's it? You just drag him out. Is he alive? Is he dead? What the HELL is going on?"

The necromancer appeared unphased as he closed and locked the door.

"I told you not to waste the food on him," Tomus said.

I saw red. Raging, I jumped on Tomus, pounding my fist into his face. The larger boy threw me off, rolled to his feet, and drew his wand.

"COME ON PRINCEY! SHOW ME WHAT YOU GOT!"

Drawing my wand, I circled him looking for an opening. Matching my every move, Tomus brandished his wand toward my head. He drew back to strike just as Pourous stepped between us.

"KNOCK IT OFF! BOTH OF YOU, STOP!"

Seething in anger, my heart pounded like a blacksmith's hammer in my head.

"Banger is gone," Pourous said. "There is nothing we can do about that. Taking it out on each other will only make us weaker. Box your damn WANDS!"

Tomus lowered his guard. I was still tempted to leap over Pourous and crown the bastard. Tomus retreated to a corner to sulk. I moved as far away from him as I could.

"You just held the wand a lot longer than twenty breaths," Pourous said.

There was distrust in his eyes. I needed to come clean.

"I have a confession. I've been able to hold it for forty-two breaths. I didn't want to say anything. I was afraid it might discourage you."

"You just held it longer than forty-two. It was probably more like sixty or seventy. It didn't even seem to affect you."

I looked down at my palm. It was usually red after an attempt, but not this time. My palm looked normal and there was no residual pain.

"I was too angry to think about the pain. Maybe that's the secret—rage. No. That can't be it. Lord Whispa was the only necromancer in history who could ever hold two wands at once. I've seen him hold dual wands many times. He never looked angry. In fact, he seemed quite calm."

"Maybe so, but I think I'm going to experiment with anger," Pourous said. "Maybe it can work for me."

I made another attempt later that sun. I tried to simulate my rage but only managed thirty-eight.

That night I was jolted from a light sleep by someone scurrying around in the dark. A strange crackling noise split the air.

"GOT IT!"

"Yeah," barked Pourous, "great shot."

"Got what?"

I couldn't see anything in the pitch black.

"Banger's blood attracted a rat and I just nailed its ass," Tomus said. "I'm still angry at you, but I'll still share."

"You're going to eat the rat! Are you crazy?"

"What's wrong Princey, too high and mighty to eat a rat?"

I felt a hand on my shoulder.

"Come on, Timikia," Pourous whispered. "It's not often we're lucky enough to get a rat. The extra meat will do you good."

"It's a rat. It's probably crawling with disease. I'm not going to eat that."

"Have it your way, Princey. More for the rest of us," Tomas said.

The two of them started tearing the hide off the poor creature. The sound of it turned my stomach. There was no way I was going to eat a rat. Slumping down on the wall, I wept. I was worn down by despair. I missed my warm bed. I wanted a hot bath. I needed my Mother. Lord Whispa was right to hide the knowledge of this place from me. If I had known, I never would have signed up for this. My civility was being stripped away. Tomus had been here for winters, but I couldn't imagine that. I was concerned my physical and mental strength was failing me.

On sun twelve, I ate a rat. I can still taste the bristly hairs stuck in my teeth. The whole time I was eating it, I imagined the squealing echoes of the little beast. But I was so hungry, I couldn't help myself. Twelve suns ago, I was a prince. Now, I was barely human. For the first time in a while, I wasn't hungry. My stomach was content. But still, I ate a rat.

The bottom flap of the door opened and food bowls slid into the room.

"Does anyone want to quit?"

"I-I- ..."

Tomus and Pourous's eyes widened.

"I-I-I- ..."

"Out with it, boy. I haven't got all sun."

"I ... don't."

The guard closed the flap and latched it. My heart was sinking at the thought of spending one more sun in this hellhole. May the powers have mercy on my soul.

Chapter #5

A Way Out

Sun sixty-three, or was it four? I wasn't quite sure anymore. Just as Tomus had predicted, I had all but stopped talking to the others. I was up to eighty-three breaths, but my progress was slowing. In the end, anger didn't help much. There were minor advances, but all too soon the improvements faded. At my current pace, I calculated it would take me two winters to complete my task. I used to be concerned about eating rats. My standards had lowered to eating bugs—live ones. I barely noticed their twitching legs as I swallowed them whole.

Memories kept me sane. Dreams of riding my horse on the palace grounds flooded my mind. Thoughts of roaming through the gardens in the spring overtook the boredom. The roses were always so fragrant. My life was awesome and I never appreciated it. Not really. I marched right on by, never noticing the sun shimmering on the lake. What I would give for one sun back home, playing with the hounds.

I tried to remember everything Lord Whispa had taught me. I was searching for any tiny detail that might help me escape from this place of sorrow. He always spoke in metaphors, symbolism, and riddles. Half the time he seemed to be rambling. Everyone said he was a great man, a great necromancer. Was he? Or was he a crazy old fool? I remembered an absolute nutty thing he tried to share with me on a hunting trip. We spotted a pack of wolves attacking a fawn. Quite grisly, but I had seen worse. Lord Whispa saw the event as amazing.

"Notice," he explained, "how the fawn is not crying out in pain. It's in shock. Shock is a gift to all creatures large and small. A gift even to man. It stops the fawn from living through the horror of the wolves' fangs. The fawn feels the teeth, but no longer experiences it as pain. The pain has become something else. Something else entirely."

The pain has become something else entirely. What a crock of …

The pain has become something else? The pain has become something else. THE PAIN HAS BECOME SOMETHING ELSE! That's it. That was the secret he attempted to share with me. If I feel it without letting my body experience it as pain, I could hold the wand forever.

My fingers fumbled with the latch. Almost tearing the box open, I grabbed the little stick.

"One … two … three …"

Imagining the pain as a waterfall rushing over my body quenched it. The feeling was still there, but the experience was different. My breath and heartbeat settled. I burnished a smile.

"Fifty-four … fifty-five …"

The lizard skull on the wand's crown twisted to stare at me. Hallucination? Reality? What difference did it make?

"Ninety-seven … ninety-eight …"

With the pain returning, I imagined colors swirling around me like dancing autumn leaves.

"One forty-two … one forty-three …"

Opening its mouth, the lizard skull hissed in anger. I laughed at the hallucination. Or was it real?

"Two o'two … two o'three …"

Its eye sockets glowed red with hate. If bones could sneer, that's what the skull was doing.

You're not going to beat me this sun, you stupid little reptile, I thought. The pain was creeping in. I was losing it. *Just a little longer*, rang through my thoughts.

"Three twenty-eight … three twenty-nine …"

The echoes of my scream alerted the others.

"Three forty-nine … three-fifty …"

The lizard was howling in defiance. The wand launched from my hand as I could take it no longer. I balled up my fist, as my arm convulsed. The mantra—*No Pain*—was flashing through my brain.

"Three sixty-three." Pourous was shocked. "How?"

A gash on my palm was oozing blood. I pressed my thumb on the wound to stop the bleeding. Surprisingly, it didn't hurt.

"I know the secret," I said, flashing a sly smile.

Over the next moon cycle, I worked on perfecting the technique. I tried to teach the others. At first, they balked at the whole idea. I had to admit, it did sound crazy. When I soared past four hundred, they took notice. I had thought the wand was the master. Now, I knew better.

Armed with hope, this place was not so bad, the food not so awful, and the floor was not so cold. I could see a light at the end of the tunnel and I was heading straight for it.

On sun ninety-six, I passed five hundred. Tomus was now a good friend. He was approaching four hundred himself and Pourous was over two hundred. I could have left anytime, but I chose to stay and help the others. When the flap opened on sun one o'seven, I knew it was time to leave.

"I, Timikia, am ready to take the test."

The flap closed. I heard the guard walk away. That was confusing, but I stayed positive. A short while later, the door opened, and in stepped Loter. His foul presence was frightening, but I was not about to let it show. All lords are intimidating, but his imposing presence was the worst. The others huddled in the corner like scared mice.

"How long can you last?" he asked my friends.

"Four hundred and twelve," Tomas uttered.

"Two eighty-one," Pourous added.

Loter peered at me with disgust.

"And you boy?"

"Over six hundred."

"How did you cheat? Are you getting help from the outside? Did someone modify your wand?"

"I have beaten the room. It's time for me to prove it."

"You've been down here less than four moons. That's impossible!"

"And yet I've done it. Care to count for yourself?" I showed no respect for him as I spoke.

"Let me see your wand," Loter demanded.

I handed him the box. Loter scrutinized the wand. He returned it to the box and handed it to me.

"Hold the wand. I'll count," he said, curling his lip with disgust.

With pride, I held my arm at full extension. Loter counted silently. I saw my friends' lips moving. At the four hundred mark, Loter looked frustrated. I reached the goal of five hundred, but Loter didn't stop me. Still, I didn't flinch. I had passed the test. He was cheating, but I didn't care. The lizard skull snarled at him as I continued. I was going to beat this jackass no matter what it took. I'd show him what peasant blood could do. At six hundred, my right eye began to twitch, but still, I held on. I shot past my personal best. At seven hundred, the guard took notice. Loter could cheat no more.

"FINE! You pass!"

Loter expected me to drop the wand in agony. Instead, I gently placed it in the box knowing it would enrage him. Waves of pain were running up and down my spine, but I refused to show weakness.

"Timikia is free to leave," Loter said to the guard. "Return him to the upper floor and find him a room."

On his way to the door, Loter stopped for one more jab.

"I don't know how you did it, but I'm going to expose you for the cheat you are. Mark my words, I'm going to expose you."

He stomped out of the room.

Pumping my fist in celebration, I spun around like a young schoolgirl.

"YEAH," Tomus screamed. He hugged me as we jumped in glee.

"You're ... you're leaving?" Pourous' voice was filled with woe. "I-I-I can't do this without you. Please don't leave."

Grabbing onto his shoulders, I placed my forehead against his.

"You don't need me. You can do this. You know the secret now. Remember what we worked on. Remember what I taught you. Don't worry, you'll be joining me upstairs soon."

Pourous gave a feeble nod.

"Get out of here, Princey," said Tomus. "Go eat a big, juicy steak. Just be sure to save one for me. I'm going to be right behind you."

"I know you will. I do not doubt that my friend. Don't take too long."

Tomus donned a huge smile. Pourous dipped his head. The guard took my arm and motioned me to the door. I waved goodbye, stepped into the hall, and watched as the guard latched the door, but this time from the other side.

Chapter #6

Fledgling?

U pon reaching the top of the stairs, the sun's warmth bathed my face. What an amazing feeling. Who would have thought I'd be excited about sunshine?

"I need some real food," I said like a rabid hound.

"First you need to clean up," said the guard. "You're not going anywhere near the kitchen smelling like that. And be sure to burn your clothes. Only the powers know what might be living in them. Just follow me."

I sniffed my shirt. It didn't seem that bad. Then again, after being in that disgusting room, I'd be lucky to smell a dead buzzard. The corridors were bustling with students dressed in fledgling gray. A few bore the guardian armor of green.

"Bathe in the waterfall. Burn your clothes in the fireplace. And put on a gray tunic when you're done."

"Am I a fledgling now?"

"You survived the room—so—yeah. Don't let it go to your head, necromancer. You're still just one step above a worthless pledge. Mealtime is over, but I'll have the attendants bring food to your room. It's the fifth one down on the right side. Try to get some sleep. The suns start early around here."

A wall of water cascaded over a tall stone barrier into the bathing room. I couldn't tell where the water was coming from and I didn't care. All I cared about was bathing. After stripping off my clothes, I threw them in the fireplace. My once expensive dressing gown was now kindling. Stepping under the waterfall was a shock to my system. It was freezing cold.

If I can eat a rat, I can do this, I told myself.

The water wasn't that bad once I got used to it. Toweling off, I reached for one of the tunics hanging up against the wall. It only came in two sizes: too big and too small. I took a big one, figuring I would grow into it. Who knows how long I would have to wear this thing? At least I could take pride in the Nocmara crest stamped on the front. Not many received this honor.

As dusk approached, I found my room. It was tiny, with a small window near the ceiling. Lo and behold, a bed with a pillow! Not a good bed, but after sleeping on a stone floor for moons, it was paradise. Tucked in the corner was a small table and chair. On the table sat a quill, ink well, lamp, and the best surprise of all—dinner. It wasn't palace food, but a thousand times better than the slop I'd been eating. I plopped down on the bed laughing with joy.

"I'm a necromancer!"

After consuming every last morsel on my plate, I drifted off to sleep.

I was awakened by a guard kicking the bedpost.

"Get up. Lord Mar wants to see you—NOW!"

Wiping the sleep from my eyes, I jumped up to follow the guard. This was going to be an exciting sun. Lord Mar probably wanted to congratulate me. The guard was already halfway down the hall before I caught up to him. It was a long trek to reach the lords' wing of the school. Massive marble pillars and gold-leaf fixtures lined the hallways in stark contrast to the fledgings' wing. Swinging a large brass knocker, the guard wrapped on the immense, orangewood door.

"I have the fledging you asked for."

"Enter," said Lord Mar from the other side.

His large office was full of books, vials, partially dismantled wands, and other necromancer items scattered everywhere. Lord Mar was seated at a massive rosewood desk. I waited as he scribed notes onto parchment.

"Have a seat, Timikia."

Lord Mar motioned to a small chair in the corner. He ignored me and kept writing. After a while, he anchored his quill and looked up.

"Under four moons. Fastest time on record. Before you, the record was just over six moons."

I smiled, "Yeah, not bad, huh?"

Lord Mar did not smile.

"Yeah, impressive. Too bad you cheated."

"Cheated? What are you talking about? How did I cheat? If anyone cheated, it was Loter. He made me hold the wand for seven hundred breaths. SEVEN HUNDRED! I only needed five hundred to pass. I covered the additional two hundred like a champion."

"The room has nothing to do with the WAND! The room proves you can endure. So far you haven't proved ANYTHING! All you've proven is that with outside help you're clever enough to cheat the system."

"Outside help? What outside help? I was locked in a stone vault the whole time."

"We interviewed your roommates. They told us how you learned the secret. Lord Whispa told you."

I turned pale as my blood ran cold.

"You want to know the worst part?" Lord Mar continued, "You infected two other pledges. If they pass now, it's only because you were their outside influence. You were THEIR cheat."

"It was just a passing comment. It was just an accident Lord Whispa said it at all."

"Lord Whispa was one of the smartest lords who ever lived. He never did anything by accident. He put that thought in your mind so you could cheat the room. If he were still alive, he'd be brought in front of the Council on charges."

The chambers fell into an awkward silence.

"Do you want to know what happened to the other necromancer, the one that got out of the room in only six moons? HE DIED! He died a horrible death during the poisoning. The room is designed to see if you can weather the storm and defeat your innermost demons. Any pledge can learn to hold the wand. Only two pledges in ten beat the room. Most quit and we want them to. Quitting the room stops them from dying later in the process. Some of our best lords were in the room for three, four, even five winters. And then there's little old you, out in three moons. Do you feel proud of yourself, now?"

I was sick. Emotions were welling up inside me.

"You have a magical soul, Timikia. I'll give you that. You proved it at your pledge test. Being a necromancer lord takes more than just magic. The room is designed to prove who is and who is not capable of it and you FAILED!"

My hands were shaking. My mouth was dry. I couldn't utter a word.

"We had an emergency meeting of the Council last night. We discussed whether you should be allowed to continue the program. The evidence of your cheating was examined and you were found lacking.

However, the real person who cheated was Lord Whispa. You just took advantage of what he told you. Your crime was sharing this information with the others. You failed to gain the value of the room and now they may as well. The proof of your crime is undeniable. But— you did not know this was a crime when you did it. It was a long discussion with a lot of heated arguments. The vote came out four to four with one lord still having yet to cast his vote."

"Which—which lord?"

I prayed he wouldn't say Loter.

"Me. It's up to me to decide your fate. What would you do if you were in my boots?"

"I-I- …"

Lord Mar was right. I screwed up everything. I didn't mean to, it just happened. But it was still my fault. My entire world was crashing down around me.

"I-I-I- … I would kick my ass out of here."

Tears streamed down my face as I dropped to my knees.

"Well—you have made a series of bad decisions since arriving at the school. Grabbing a wand, you had no business trying to hold. Allowing Lord Loter to goad you into it. Talking back to lords. Sharing classified information with pledges. Worse of all, allowing your pride to get the better of you. I can't believe how many enemies you've made since arriving. So—I have to assume your last comment is yet another example in a long string of your bad decisions. I vote you stay."

I was shocked. He smirked as if this was somehow funny.

"There is just one condition. If you ever get in the way of a pledge, or necromancer, learning a valuable lesson again, I will personally kick your ass all the way back to your palace on the hill. Do you understand me?"

I nodded in humility.

"Breathe. You look like you're going to faint."

Lord Mar helped me back into my chair.

"Do you have questions for me, young Timikia?"

"Just one."

"Go ahead."

"Sometimes in the room, when I was holding the wand, the lizard skull would move. Did I imagine that or did it really happen?"

"Excellent question," Lord Mar replied. "The answer is both."

"Both? Either I imagined it or it was real. It can't be both."

"Oh, you have so much to learn, Timikia. If you haven't figured it out yet, the wands are alive. In the past few hundred winters, we have learned to make the wands ourselves. But the best wands, the original wands, were stolen from the bowels of hell. There's a life force inside each one. You don't command the wand; the wand cooperates with you—IF it wants to. When you see it move, you only see it in your mind. No one else sees it. It's the wand's way of communicating with you. It moves of its own free will, but only in your imagination."

"How do you make it want to cooperate with you?"

"Just like Nocmara, the wand wants to see if you're worthy. The wand has its own tests. Every pledge wants to be a great necromancer. Every wand wants to be welded by a great power. That's why your father's wand was so hard for you to hold. Imagine a wand like that going from Lord Timicus, God Emperor of the Dead, to a lowly pledge. When your wand's skull moved, what did it do?"

"It howled and hissed at me."

Lord Mar smirked, "And then what happened?"

"I had a cut on my palm that was bleeding down my arm. That has never happened before or since."

"Yeah, it bit you. It probably didn't like how cocky you were becoming. Let me guess, you thought you were its master. Always remember, you are not the master of the wand. At best, it's a friend and not a terribly good friend at that. It's time for you to go back to your palace."

"What? I thought you said I could stay."

"You're not going back forever, just until you regain your strength. You'll need it for what comes next. Go home, enjoy the royal lifestyle, and return ready to work harder than you thought was possible. I expect to see you back here within a moon cycle—Necromancer Timikia."

He gave me a wink and waved me out of the room.

"Oh, one more thing," he added, "if you had begged me to stay in the program, I would have booted you out forthright. It's because you took responsibility for your actions that I'm allowing you to remain. Lord Loter wanted you out of here in the worst way. I'm taking a big chance on you. Don't let me down."

Chapter #7

Trouble at Home

W hy do barbarians have to stink so badly? You'd think when meeting with an important monarch like myself from another kingdom they'd at least bathe.

"You have to do something about this," I said, staring at the odorous diplomat.

"I'm sorry Queen Lika, but the groups that attacked your villages aren't part of the horde. There's nothing Tsar Postand can do to help. His hands are tied."

This man had to be the worst diplomat in all of Atlantis. He couldn't even lie well. But it was clear, he had mastered the art of being condescending.

"The men who attacked our villages were barbarians. Postand is the king of the barbarians," I explained.

"He is the tsar. Yes."

"Fine, the tsar, whatever—the point is he's supposed to be in charge. Is he not?"

"His excellency, Tsar Postand, lord of all the mountains, general of all the seas, commander of the sky itself is the leader of all barbarians past, present, and future," answered the diplomat.

"But he can't stop a small rag-tag band of raiders?"

"Correct."

"Well, then you'd better tell Tsar Postand that I'm giving the order this sun as queen to move two legions of my best troops to the Surdon Pass."

"THAT, my good woman, would be a very provocative move on your part."

"I've given the tsar two winters to do something—ANYTHING—about the raids and yet they continue. My men are going to keep the peace. Tell Tsar Postand that my next move will be to petition the Council of the Brotherhood to send a battalion of necromancers to the pass. I'm sure he would love to hear that."

"THAT, my good woman, would be an act of WAR!"

"Then, let's hope it doesn't come to that. My soldiers are going to slaughter any raiders we find on our land. Since they're not HIS people, he shouldn't care, RIGHT?"

"I'll share your position with my sovereign, but I do not think he will be pleased."

"I don't care if he is pleased or not. And tell your sovereign that next time he wants to negotiate, to come himself. Don't send some mouthpiece who is two turkeys short of an ox."

He snorted like a bull being neutered and stormed from my council chambers.

"That didn't sound good," said a small cracking voice from the shadows. Grabbing a letter opener off my desk, I spun to face this hidden threat. There he was, my boy. Skinny, poorly kept, and dressed in a drab gray tunic—but clearly, my boy. I ran and threw my arms around him, holding him close.

"By the powers, you're skin and bones. Weren't they feeding you?"

"Ah ... not really, no."

"We'll take care of that. I'll have Chef Cherine fix all your favorites. Why are you home so quickly? Did it not go well? Did you end up quitting? You can tell me. No matter what, you'll always be my pride and joy."

Pointing to the crest on his chest, Timikia said, "I'm a fledgling necromancer now."

"IN FOUR MOONS! Wow! That has to be some sort of record. Lord Mar must be so impressed!"

A wave of pride flowed over me. I looked into Timikia's blue eyes, which he inherited from his father. I thought I would see the pride shining back at me. Instead, his eyes were cold and concerning. What happened to the boy who had left only a few moons ago?

"Is everything all right, my son?"

"We can chat about that later. What's up with the barbarians? That didn't seem like a friendly conversation."

"Oh, they're just up to their old tricks again. They've been raiding livestock and bullying the local villagers. But it's never been this bad before."

"Should you have the villages evacuated?" said Timikia.

"The pass may no longer be a safe place for our people. But most of them have no place else to go. I'm confident that General Jaker can restore and strengthen our borders. He's a strong leader. His men will do anything for him. But enough of this. Let's get you fed and into proper clothes for a prince."

I tried to take his hand, as I had done so many times before, but he pulled away. He was gone for such a short time and yet it seemed like he had aged winters. He was quiet in both speech and step as we walked toward the kitchen. The silence was uncomfortable. When I couldn't take it any longer, I spoke up.

"So, what's been happening to you the last four moons?"

"I can't tell you."

"Oh, come on. I am not only the queen, but I'm also your mother. Surely you can tell me."

My son gave me a stern look.

"I can't share that. Don't ask me again."

The young man standing in front of me wasn't my little Timikia anymore.

Chef Cherine was surprised and delighted to see the young prince enter the kitchen.

"Prince Timikia, you're back! Let me warm up some lamb stew for you. It will just take a moment."

Grabbing a plate, Timikia spooned up some cold potatoes, sat down on the floor, and started eating. Cherine wasn't sure how to handle this new development. After several awkward moments, I sat down on the floor next to him.

"Tell me more about the barbarians," he said. "You seem to be hiding something from me."

I thought this was strange. Timikia was never interested in politics before. This was new territory for us.

"Not here. Too many ears. Follow me."

He followed me to the dining hall, still carrying his half-eaten plate of potatoes. I sat at the head of the table, expecting Timikia to take his usual place on the far side. Instead, he sat right next to me.

"Tell me," said Timikia.

This was not the sort of burden a mother should place on her young son, but the boy was dead and this man had taken his place. I decided to share everything.

"About fifty winters ago, the barbarians engaged in a violent war against the demon tribes. The barbarians had a powerful army—many well-trained, well-armed men. At great cost, they beat the demons back. Afterward, they were so depleted they only played a small part in local affairs. That is until about a winter ago. They started raiding with ever-increasing brutality. We fear they are building another great army. All kingdoms on the barbarians' borders are on heightened alert. The Brotherhood is not the power they once were. They were in decline even in the time of your father. The situation has not improved since his death. I've sent spies into the barbarians' lands. None have returned. I assume they were caught and executed."

"Can we afford to send two legions to the Surdon Pass? Wouldn't that leave our border with the Sorceri grossly undefended?" asked Timikia.

All those winters as a boy, when I thought he was just playing in the corner, he had been listening.

"The Sorceri have few troops on our border. They've already repositioned their forces to address the greater barbarian threat. In fact, I have been considering approaching them with an alliance proposal."

"Are you kidding? An alliance with the Sorceri? They have been the dreaded enemies of the Brotherhood for hundreds of winters," said Timikia.

"More like thousands of winters. But the enemy of an enemy—"

"Considering their hatred for us, could we trust them in battle?"

"Your father fought alongside the mother of the current High Mage. They fought to defeat a bug. The situation is not without precedence. The barbarians wouldn't dare take us both on."

"Plus, we don't want the Sorceri to create an alliance with the barbarians," said Timikia. "That would be a disaster."

I was taking war council from a twelve-winters-old boy, but I was gaining respect for my son's growing wisdom.

"These things take time to play out. Enough of this talk for now. Let's find you some cleaner clothes."

Over the next ten suns, I noticed glimmers of the old Timikia. He was smiling again. Despite eating only two small meals a sun he started putting on weight. Once a picky eater, now he would wolf down anything.

On sun fifteen, he began returning to his favorite hobbies: riding his prized horse, reading books from his father's extensive library, and even painting a bit. Just as I thought life was returning to normal, a communique arrived.

I found him studying the letter in his room. The boy was gone again, and the man had returned.

"What's it say?" I inquired.

"It's from Nocmara. They are requesting my return."

"Do you feel prepared?"

"There is no way to prepare. I have no idea what is coming next. If it's half as hard as the last test, I question my resolve. Did you know?"

"Know what?"

"That Lord Whispa was cheating for me?"

"What! Lord Whispa passed on to the other side two winters ago. How could he have possibly helped you?"

"He was feeding me information I was not supposed to know. A piece of that information almost got me kicked out of the school."

"My dear, Lord Whispa was a man of great integrity. He was your father's mentor, right-hand man, and best friend for over a hundred winters. When your father died, while you were still in my womb, he took over and helped raise you. He loved you like a son. He would never do anything to hurt you."

"He loved me like a son. Maybe that was the problem. He was supposed to be my teacher, not my father. Fathers want to spare their children hardships. Maybe that's what he was thinking. The danger is that I don't know how much more of this information is in my head. Loter is just waiting for me to screw up. I was hoping that being my father's son would buy me many friends, but instead, it has created many enemies."

"You don't have to follow in your father's footsteps," I said, desperate to comfort him. "If it's too hard, you can always quit."

Timikia pounded his fist onto the table. It shook violently from the blow.

"STOP SAYING THAT! Everyone keeps saying that. Just quit! Just quit! Just quit! I'm never going to quit, NEVER! I'm going to become a guardian and then a lord. I'm going to sit on the council SOME SUN! No one is going to stop me. Not you. Not Whispa. Not even Loter."

Timikia slammed the desk into the wall.

"Some sun, Loter is going to fear ME!"

"By the powers—you're emoting."

"WHAT?"

His eyes emitted a bright blue fog. He panted as a man possessed.

"You're emoting," I said again.

Timikia's anger turned to confusion. The fog began dissipating.

"Beginning fledglings don't emote."

"I swear to you. You were."

"I need to return to Nocmara, this sun. I need to learn how to use this power. No—to control this power—before it's too late."

Chapter #8

First Sun of Class

The crimson sky bathed the gray stones of Nocmara as I approached. It was strange being treated, once again, with complete indifference. Back at Palace City, I was revered. Soldiers and peasants alike bowed to me. Here I was a lowly fledgling. The guards barely glanced up as I passed, as if I was a chicken being brought in for the morning's meal. Lords strolled around Atlantis like gods. Last sun, the palace staff gushed over my necromancer tunic. Here, just another fledgling, better off ignored.

Sconces illuminated the hallway as I returned to my room. Fumbling in the dark, I located the small lamp. It took ten sparks to light it as if it hadn't been used in winters. I found my itinerary laying on the floor. Battle class was to begin at first light. Battle class sounded interesting, in stark contrast to the boredom of the room. Reading class was next, which excited me. The palace library had tons of wonderful books due to my father being an avid collector. The library of Nocmara must be amazing. The third item on the list was simply a question mark followed by a hall name and room number. That seemed odd and piqued my curiosity.

The bed was much harder than my goose-down mattress at the palace. Still, it was better than a stone floor. With the excitement of the next sun looming, I worried I would not sleep. I was wrong. I didn't even remember falling asleep.

The sun was already in the sky when I woke up. I WAS LATE! I threw on my boots, grabbed my wand box, and shot out the door. The hallway was empty. Everyone else had started their sun. Panicked, I ran to the open court. Dozens of fledglings were already assembled. They were all older than me. Some of them looked more like men than boys. A few had beards. They were all standing on their left legs, with their right foot pressed against their left knee, like a flock of sleeping flamingos. I scurried to the end of the formation, fumbling to mimic their posture. It was far more difficult than it seemed.

"Look who decided to grace us with his presence," the training lord remarked to the class. "It's Prince Timikia, son of the Great Lord Timicus, heir to the throne of Surdon."

He got right in my face. I could smell the meat he had eaten for breakfast.

"And you know what all that means here, boy? Nothing. Absolutely nothing."

"And what do we do when someone is late to class?" he barked at the boy next to me.

"You instruct him, Lord Vicar!" said the fledgling. His tone was loud and respectful.

"Yes, fledging, you are absolutely correct. I instruct them."

Drawing his wand, he jabbed me in the chest. It burned so badly I fell to the ground.

"What the HELL! Why did you do that?"

He grabbed a handful of my tunic, lifting me until I was nose to nose with him.

"You don't like my instruction methods? Then quit! Otherwise, shut up and get back in formation."

He hauled me to my feet. He was strong for a frail-looking old man. He got right back in my face.

"Trust me, you're going to hate me before you get out of my class and I don't give a damn. If you're late again, I will make this instruction look mild. Do you understand?"

I nodded.

"The correct response is YES, LORD VICAR!"

He held the wand near my chest. The close proximity was irritating the burn. I wanted to check on my wound, but I returned to standing on one leg or at least making an attempt.

"Yes, Lord Vicar."

"LOUDER!"

"YES, LORD VICAR!"

The sun crossed to mid-sky and still we all just stood on one leg, not uttering a word. The muscles in my left leg and back were burning. How could something so simple be so hard?

"What's wrong, fledgling?" Lord Vicar commented, "Having troubles?"

He was back in my face waiting for a reply.

"It is harder than it appears, my Lord. I'm trying my best."

I prayed that was the right thing to say. I was relieved as he turned to walk away. Unfortunately, I was too stupid for my own good and I continued to speak. "I don't understand how this has anything to do with battle, my Lord," I said.

Once again, he spoke to the fledging next to me.

"The Prince here doesn't understand how any of this relates to battle. Do you understand, fledgling?"

"YES, LORD VICAR, I DO!"

"Hmmm … That's good. If only this worthless fledgling was as smart as you."

Without warning, Lord Vicar turned and kicked me in the chest. I bolted to the ground. He jumped on top of me, using his knees to pin my arms. He held his wand up next to my cheek. It wasn't touching me, but I could feel its power burning my face.

"If I was a demon, you'd be defeated right now, or I would be eating your flesh while you helplessly watched. If you had better balance, you wouldn't have fallen. You would have been in a position to defend yourself. You are one stupid fledgling. Wise up or you'll be dinner for a demon some sun."

He addressed the group.

"I'm sick of all of you, useless sacks of meat. Class dismissed!"

Several fledglings walked past me snickering. None of them helped me to my feet or showed any remote sign of empathy. My leg and back ached, causing me to walk with a limp. My cheek was swollen from Lord Vicar's latest assault. My chest still burned. Pulling my tunic back, I examined a charred mark on my chest, the size of my fist.

Reading class sounded so much better than this shit. I expected to see a massive library. Instead, I found just another small, cold, gray stone room. Ten fledglings sat at their desks, each with a single old book. No lords, just a couple of guardians overseeing things. One of them pointed to a desk in the corner. I limped over and sat down. It felt good not to be standing anymore. The guardian opened up a large cabinet at the front of the room and removed a massive book about the length of my forearm and half as thick. He plopped it on my desk, blowing off the thick layer of dust straight into my face. My chest throbbed as I choked. He flipped open the cover and began to explain things.

"This spell book has been selected specifically for you. Every sun you will return here and study the book. You will read it, learn from it, and memorize it. If you last long enough, you'll add your notes to it. When you pass on to the other side, this book will be presented to another fledgling so your knowledge will be preserved. Guard it with your life. It must never fall into the wrong hands."

I gazed at the first page, but it was nothing but gibberish. A bunch of unrelated letters strung together with no spaces.

"Excuse me," I said, "I'm fluent in four languages, but I don't recognize any of this. What language is this?"

"It's code. Every necromancer creates his own personal code to protect his spells and research."

"Well—what's the code. How do I read this?"

"That's for you to figure out. If the book was used by multiple necromancers, it could have several different codes. Good luck," he snickered. "You'll need it."

What the hell? This sun kept getting worse. The fledgling next to me was about sixteen or seventeen winters old. Maybe he had experience he would be willing to share with me.

"Hi. Have you figured out your code?"

"Mostly."

That was hopeful.

"How many pages have you translated so far?"

"As of this morning, four."

"Four? How long have you been working on it?"

"Two winters."

Oh, crap! My book had to be two thousand pages. The words "I QUIT," flashed through my brain.

"Pull yourself together, Timikia," I whispered to myself.

I tried everything—character substitution, letter rearrangement, word displacement, but nothing seemed to work. By the end of the class, I had made no progress at all. Tucking the book under my arm and grabbing my wand box, I limped to my next class, the question mark class.

It was the smallest classroom yet. Four student desks were aligned in a row with a huge desk for the instructor at the front of the room. I could only see the very top of a lord's hood over the back of a massive leather chair.

"Have a seat," said the lord not even bothering to turn around.

I took the seat farthest from the door, figuring others would be joining me soon, but no other fledglings came in. It was just me. The lord never turned his chair to face me. The sun crossed the sky and the lord never moved. Finally, I asked a question, half expecting to be struck with a wand.

"What am I supposed to be doing?"

"Silence! I'll let you know when I need something from you, fledgling."

It was rude but better rude than a wand to the chest. And so, I sat. My stomach growled. I had missed the opening meal, if there was one. My mind turned to my spell book. I lifted it onto the desk. Just as I was about to turn the cover, the lord chimed in.

"Focus on what you are supposed to learn in this class. Study on your own time. Don't waste mine. Close the book."

How did he know what I was doing? I put the book back on the floor. What was I supposed to be learning? Maybe that this oakwood chair makes my butt hurt? More sun drifted by. The boredom was worse than the room. I closed my eyes and laid my head on the desk.

"WAKE UP! There will be NO sleeping in my classroom!"

He always knew what I was doing. I waited, and waited, and waited. When the sun was low in the sky the lord spun his chair around to address me.

"I am Lord Pinge. Ask me an intelligent question?"

"Umm … how do you raise the dead?"

"I said an intelligent question."

"All right, what's the best way to create a bone weapon?"

"I said an intelligent question."

I thought about it for a tad. He clearly didn't want anything to do with spells.

"What is the true value of seeing the other side?"

"If you don't have any intelligent questions, come back tomorrow and we will try again."

He got up and left me sitting there in total confusion. After gathering my things, I headed back to my room. On the way, I heard many chattering voices. I followed the sound to a large dining hall. Nocmara was so massive I had not seen this section before. Fledglings and guardian instructors were gathered for the nightly meal. Finally, food arrived. I grabbed a tray and got in line. Food was plentiful, and for the most part, it looked pretty good. I made my selections and started back to the tables. It was hard to balance the tray, my book, and the wand. I scanned the room for friendly faces. The guardians were off to themselves, not interacting with the fledglings. Lord Mar told me to keep a low profile, so I thought it was best to ignore them. A group of four boys were laughing with each other. I hadn't heard much laughter since arriving at Nocmara. All four were older than me, of course, but they looked friendly enough. They stopped eating and stared at me as I placed my tray on their table.

"I can leave if you want," I said after an awkward pause.

The oldest one, maybe eighteen winters old, snickered.

"First sun?"

"Uh-huh."

"Rough sun?"

"Yeah … pretty much."

"Don't worry about it. The first sun is rough for everyone."

A red-headed boy of about sixteen winters started laughing.

"Yeah," he chimed in, "and then it only gets worse."

The others laughed with him.

"The name's Pertwee," said the oldest after a good chuckle. "That's Patheranica," pointing to the redhead, "but everyone calls him Flames. That's Mertu and Zip. His real name is Zippooh, but he hates that. Don't call him that."

"I'm Timikia."

"You're Timikia? The guy that got out of the room in four moons? Hey guys, we're dining with a celebrity. It took me a winter and a half."

"It took me two and a half," added Flames. "Welcome to Nocmara, kid, or as we like to call it—"

"HELL," all four said in unison. That prompted more laughter.

"You know what?" Pertwee asked. "We could use a sidekick like you in our little group. You want to join up?"

"Sure."

It was the first sign of kindness since I arrived.

"You may have noticed that no one tells you shit in this crazy school. Most of the time, it's like walking around in a blind alley. Let me make it easier for you. Got any questions?"

"My battle class starts at the crack of dawn—"

All the boys moaned, "Oh, Lord Vicar's class."

"How do you wake up on time for it? The window lets in so little light; it doesn't make me stir."

"You just ask one of the attendants to wake you up."

"IT'S THAT EASY?"

"I told you, nobody tells you shit around here. Anything else?"

"Is this the only meal of the sun?"

"Noooo, they have breakfast before the first class," Pertwee said. "But you have to get up early enough to eat it. I'll tell you what, you show me where your room is and I'll wake you up tomorrow in plenty of time for chow. Stick with me kid and I'll show you the ropes."

A ray of hope. I had made a friend.

Chapter #9

How Useless School

"**W**ake up you worthless fledgling."

A violent kick to my headboard jolted me awake. My eyes struggled to focus.

"It's time to get something to eat."

Despite the harsh words, his voice was cheerful. Rubbing the sleep from my eyes, I saw a dark outline silhouetted by the hallway's lamps.

"Pertwee! You scared the crap out of me."

"No time to waste. It's the second sun of the new moon, so pancakes and pigs. First come, first serve, so get your lazy ass up. You might want to grab your book and wand while you're at it. It's a long way back from the dining hall."

I grabbed my stuff and shot out after my new friend. Pertwee was well down the hall by the time I caught up.

"Sleep well?" he inquired.

"Yeah! I was exhausted."

Pertwee snickered, "Yeah, everyone sleeps pretty well around here. It doesn't get any easier. By the end of the sun, you're bushed. Sort of makes you wonder why anyone would sign up for this crap in the first place. Doesn't it? Though, I've heard it gets better once you make guardian."

"How close are you?"

"Who knows. It's all up to the warden," he said with a laugh. "I mean headmaster of Nocmara. Maybe a couple more winters."

Pertwee was the first student to make me laugh. He always had a smile on his face and a jab at the ready.

"How long have you been here so far?"

"Seven winters give or take. Although it seems like twenty."

We grabbed our trays and got in line. Most of the other students had beat us to it. The pancakes did look good. They were smeared with blackberry jam and butter. I took four and moved on to the next station. I was wondering what pigs were. My imagination ran to ugly places. What a relief to find out they were sausages.

"Look for the more cooked ones," Pertwee advised. "They'll be less juicy, but your stomach will thank you later."

Taking his advice, I speared three that were on the blackish side. I followed him to the dining hall where we met up with Flames and Zip. They were halfway through their meal already.

"Where is Mertu?" I inquired.

"He doesn't always eat with us," Pertwee explained. "Half the time he is hunkered down in a corner someplace studying his book."

"He hasn't even broken the code yet," Flames added.

"How long has he been trying?"

"About three winters. I've heard if you haven't read your book by then, there are discussions about booting you out. He's a good guy, just not a good necromancer. It's taking him so long. Must be costing his family a fortune. I was asking around about you last night. Turns out, you're royalty."

"Not here I'm not."

Pertwee snickered, "come on Timikia, what's your back story. Out with it."

"Truly, I don't think it matters anymore. I'm just a lowly fledgling like everyone else who is stupid enough to attempt this. All my privilege has done for me so far is cause trouble. I've made some powerful enemies."

"Enemies? Like who?"

"Loter."

"LORD LOTER?"

"Yeah."

"The Lord Loter that sits on the council of nine? That Lord Loter?"

"Yeah."

"What did you do to ruffle his feathers?"

"I'm not exactly sure, but he definitely has it in for me."

"Whoa! Maybe you should sit someplace else. Some of your bad vibrations might rub off on the rest of us."

Pertwee was probably right. I might bring grief to everyone around me. Politically, I was in way over my head.

"I understand. I'll move."

Frowning, I stood and picked up my tray.

"Sit down! I'm just poking you. Are you kidding? It's going to be WAY too much fun to watch you try and navigate this place. I wouldn't want to miss a front-row seat for that. It's almost dawn. Eat up, you don't want to be late to Lord Vicar's class."

He was right about that. My chest was still aching. I took one more bite and sprinted off. Lord Vicar was nowhere in sight when I arrived. I chose a spot in the formation near the entrance. I wanted to make sure I was noticed. Upon arriving, Lord Vicar spotted me straight off.

"How are you feeling this morning, Timikia?"

He finger-flicked my chest in the worst spot. I fought hard not to flinch.

"I'm doing well, Lord Vicar. Thank you for asking."

He flashed me a laughing smile and moved on. The other fledglings filed in and chose their positions. Lord Vicar addressed us as the morning light streamed over the court walls.

"This morning you meaningless peons, who are not even worthy of being here, we will be working on position two. Begin!"

My knowledge of positions was nonexistent. Everyone else went straight into flamingo again, only this time on the right leg. I followed suit. Just another sun of stumbling like an idiot. Ten breaths later, a fledgling ran into the courtyard desperate to find a place in the formation. He ended up four spots to the left and one row behind me.

"Well, well, well," Lord Vicar bellowed, "it seems Simatto hasn't figured out when the sun comes up."

Lord Vicar got right in his face.

"I believe this is your third time being late. Is that correct, fledgling?"

Turning white, the boy shivered.

"I was barely late, my Lord. Barely."

"That wasn't my question. Was it? It seems you're also hard of hearing. I'll repeat the question a little louder. Is this, or is this not, your third time?"

"Yes, it is. I lost track of the sun studying my book."

Lord Vicar walked my way. Why was he walking over to me? I hadn't done anything. His face was a butterfly wing's distance from my cheek.

"Fledgling Timikia, I think you have had some experience with a similar situation. What do I do when someone is late to MY class? MY CLASS!"

Vicar was right about one thing—I hated him already. I didn't want to answer, worrying that anything I said would be wrong.

"You instruct them, my Lord."

"Yes, that's right. You are absolutely right. You learn quickly for a useless fledgling and I stress the word 'useless.'"

Vicar drew his wand. Holding my breath, I prepared for the worst. Instead, Vicar moved away toward the other boy.

"No, no—please my Lord. It won't happen again. I'll stay after class. I'll do a double class. It won't happen again, I promise."

"Oh, I'm pretty sure it won't happen again."

Vicar grabbed the boy's hair and jammed the wand under his jaw. The scream was horrific. I could see the boy's skull glowing through his skin. He fell to the ground twitching. Then, he grew still.

"Eyes forward fledglings! There is nothing to see here! If any of you move a muscle to aid him, you will be next."

The boy lay motionless for quite some time. Was he dead? After a twelfth-sun, he began to stir. Gradually, he returned to his feet, attempting to form position two. His skin was clammy. His eyes were dull. I didn't dare look around, but I wondered how the others felt about this near homicidal act.

Time passed in silence, the quiet only broken by Vicar's occasional insults. When at last he dismissed us, the injured boy collapsed on all fours. He hurled up his pancakes and pigs. I tried to help, but he waved me off. Despite his pain, he was looking out for others. Reluctantly, I left him hovering over a pool of his own vomit.

During reading class, concentration was difficult. I was haunted by the image of that boy. This is a den of lunatics. I could be home in my warm bed, with a book I could actually read. Instead, I was being tortured and watching others receive the same horrible treatment. Maybe quitting wasn't such a bad idea. It would be so easy. Two simple words and I would be out of this hell.

After accomplishing nothing, I moved on to the next class. Similar to the sun before, I arrived to find Lord Pinge with his back to me. I took a seat and waited, and waited, and waited. What a waste of my time. I could be practicing holding my wand, trying to crack the code, or even standing on one leg. Anything would be better than this. As expected, when the light started dwindling, Lord Pinge spun his chair around.

"Ask me an intelligent question?"

I thought to myself, *Here we go again. I don't understand the point of any of this.*

"Who used my wand before me?"

"I said an intelligent question."

"How do they decide if and when a fledgling becomes a guardian?"

"An intelligent question, please."

The events of this sun rained in on my soul. My thoughts darkened as I asked the question that was truly on my mind.

"Why is it considered acceptable for a lord to attempt to kill a fledgling?"

Lord Pinge grew quiet. He had a blank look on this face. I didn't break eye contact. I needed this question answered.

"Well, if you don't have any intelligent questions, come back tomorrow and we'll try again."

I was seething in anger. It seemed like the lords could do whatever they wanted, whenever they wanted, and to whomever they wanted. Even murder seemed to be a line they were willing to cross.

Arriving at the dining hall, I sat with my friends. Pertwee was his usual jokester self, but I didn't find him funny this sun. I returned to my quarters and had a fitful sleep.

Chapter #10

The Turning Point

I learned to keep my head down. Standing in the back row drew less attention from Vicar. The less the better. I never met anyone so negative and cruel. Battle class was useless. When are we going to train for battle? All we do is pose like an eagle, stand on our heads, put a foot behind our backs. The endless, pointless tasks just kept coming. After about two moons of this nonsense, I was greeted by a pleasant surprise.

"Tomas! You made it," I said, crying in glee.

"Princey! Yeah, here I am, ugly gray tunic and all. I'm excited to learn how to fight."

"Ah … yeah … whatever. It's good to see you."

"I have to thank you for that, Timikia. I owe you much. I wouldn't have made it without your advice. Before you arrived, I was closer to the breaking point than I cared to admit."

That comment depressed me. It's exactly what Lord Mar told me would happen. Even so, seeing Tomus again filled me with cheer.

"What's going on with Porous. How long before he joins us?"

Tomas's smile faded.

"Porous didn't make it. He quit about ten suns after you left. He didn't even talk to me about it. I think you were the only thing keeping him going. Once you were gone, he lost all hope. From what he told us about his father, I fear he traded one bad place for another. He didn't even say goodbye."

I mourned the loss of my friend. The odds of seeing him again were bleak. Tomas donned a forced smile in an attempt to lighten the mood.

"Any advice you can give me about battle class?"

"Umm … yeah. Don't ask any questions."

After class, Tomas and I chatted briefly. I told him about my new group of friends and invited him to sit with us that evening. I felt responsible for Tomas. After all, I had helped him cheat his way out of the room.

Reading class was another complete failure. As sun after sun passed overhead, I still could not break the code. I had yet to translate a single word. I tried to get help from other fledglings and even the guardian attendants, but they refused. They claimed it was my responsibility. If only I could learn one spell, just one, I would finally feel like a real necromancer. I felt like a pretender. What a joke. I'm the son of the great Lord Timicus and I can't even stand on one leg.

The moons passed by, six in total since returning to the school. It was no surprise that I was summoned to Lord Mar's council chambers. I had made no progress whatsoever. Fledglings are judged by their headway. Sometimes they don't return from these meetings. Mertu didn't.

Lord Mar stared at me with a furrowed brow. Was my time up? Had I endured all the pain, boredom, confusion, and frustration, only to be sent home in disgrace?

"I'm disappointed in you, Timikia. I've received discouraging reports. Your performance in battle class is substandard. You haven't cracked your code. You haven't even learned your very first and most important lesson."

"What lesson is that?"

"You cheated the room. You didn't learn the lesson of the room. That lack of understanding is weighing you down like an anchor. You're sinking fast and many have noticed."

"What … lesson? That under the right conditions I'll eat rats and bugs? That I can sleep night after night on a stone floor? That I can bear a wand for five hundred breaths? What was I supposed to learn? WHAT LESSON?"

Lord Mar was annoyed by my outburst.

"Not only didn't you learn the answer, you don't even know the question. Lord Loter wants us to dismiss you. There are others on the council that tend to agree with him. But as headmaster, that decision is mine and mine alone. Do you even want to be a necromancer lord?"

I slowly nodded, "Yes."

"Why? After all, you'd still be a prince. Seems like a pretty good deal to me. Many a boy would kill to trade places with you."

I thought long and hard about my answer before I spoke.

"Lord Whispa told me story after story about the deeds of the great necromancer lords, the battles, the rescues, and the political triumphs. They seemed like gods guiding history. But the story I remember most is the one about my parents. Just before my mother was about to be dragged to hell by a demon bug, my father gave his life to save her. But if he hadn't been a necromancer lord, it wouldn't have mattered how brave he was or how much he loved her. It would have all been meaningless. A normal man, even a great warrior, would be stomped into the mud by that hideous thing. In that single moment, he saved his love, their unborn son, created a queen, saved a kingdom, and inspired me to follow in his footsteps. Why do I want to be a necromancer lord? Because one sun … one sun … I may have a chance to make that kind of difference. Like my father before me, I want to be ready."

After opening up my soul and pouring it out, I felt spent.

"I'm going to give you one more chance, Timikia. You have five suns to figure out the lesson of the room. If you can do that, you may stay. I wish you the best of luck."

He waved me out of his chambers. I was numb. Pertwee, Flames, Zip, and Tomus were gathered outside my room awaiting the news.

"What happened?" Pertwee asked.

"I have five suns. Five suns to figure out the lesson of the room. If I don't figure it out, I'm dismissed."

"WHAT?" Tomas questioned. "You cleared the room. You helped me clear the room. You cleared the room in four moons. That's a record time. YOU'RE TIMIKIA, the son of the great Lord Timicus. You saw! You saw the other side as a pledge. As a pledge! You're the best of all of us. There is no way they can kick you out."

"And yet they might. I cheated the room. I'm afraid I may have to pay for my arrogance. I have no idea what the lesson is."

"What lesson?" asked Flames. "The room was just about holding the wand."

"I guess there is more to it, or so they tell me."

"Well, if there is a lesson, I don't know what it is either," Pertwee said.

"Maybe you can't put it into words, but you learned the lesson nonetheless. You all did. I have five suns to catch up."

I spent three suns obsessed with finding the answer. Everything else was a distraction. I relived every moment in the room over and over again. What did I miss? It had to be something profound, something important, but I came up with nothing.

Sitting in Lord Pinge's class on the fourth sun, I wrangled with the question. *Let's go over it again*, I thought. *I would wake up in the morning. Be hungry. Make my first attempt to hold the wand. Be hungry. Rub the pain out of my shoulder. Be hungry. Get impatient waiting for my next attempt.*

The clouds parted and the sun shone down. I would get impatient. Impatient for the pain to stop. Impatient for the next attempt. Impatient for the food to arrive. I spent four moons being impatient and I was still doing it. Impatient to learn to fight. Impatient to crack the code. I was always impatient.

Right at that moment, Lord Pinge spun his chair around. It felt like a sign from the powers.

"Ask me an intelligent question."

"How do I learn to have patience?"

A large smile formed on Lord Pinge's face. It was his first in all these moons.

"That, my young apprentice, is an excellent question. Come back tomorrow and we'll start working on the answer."

He stood, patted me on the head like a puppy, and left without another word.

The next morning, I was summoned to Lord Mar's council chambers. I entered with a ray of hope. Before I reached his desk, he started quizzing me.

"What have you learned?"

"I've spent the last winter at Nocmara wasting my time. Always trying to do everything quicker, faster, better, and failing all the while. I have been questioning the process, frustrated with the methods, pressing to get more and more knowledge in a shorter and shorter time. I was never present in the moment. I was never content with where I was. I failed to absorb the wisdom of the necromancer lord standing right in front of me. I didn't have the patience to understand. The faster I tried to go, the less progress I made. Without patience, I could have the most magical soul in the world and I'd still be a lousy student. Being a necromancer is more about discipline than magic. I missed that lesson."

Lord Mar nodded, "Yes, that is the lesson of the room. It's never been worded better. I was ready to let you stay even before you walked in. Last sun, Lord Pinge gave you a glowing report. There is no one better than Lord Pinge to teach patience. He has patience to spare. After all, he spent the last six moons sitting with you hoping for a good question."

"Wait—doesn't he do that with all the fledglings?"

"Did you see any other fledglings in your class? That class was designed specifically for you. I wasn't ready to give up on you and neither was he. Last sun, you gave us hope. You've turned the corner of your education. Now, get back out there and show us who you really are. What you can really do."

Chapter #11

The Code Secret

Closing the book cover, I fought my frustration, but still no progress. This patience thing was difficult. In truth, my mind was too occupied with the question mark class. Up until now, I knew exactly what to expect. This sun, I could be walking into almost anything.

"Welcome, Timikia," said Lord Pinge. "Put your things on the far desk and come sit by me."

I complied feeling a twinge of separation anxiety. The wand wasn't quite my friend, but we had learned to trust each other.

He dipped a thin glass rod into an earthenware cup.

"Are you ready to learn patience?"

"Yes."

I was ready—nervous, but ready.

Raising the rod, he drew a single drop of liquid along its stem.

"Raise your hand in front of your face. Palm down. Relax and just let your fingers hang naturally."

He moved the rod gingerly toward my fingers. I jerked my hand away.

"What is that?"

"Do you want to learn patience or not?"

Both yes and no were terrifying choices. I had been poked, jabbed, stabbed, and abused. How was I to trust? Was it necromancer poison or something worse? It wasn't green, so not poison. However, it could be "something worse." His expression gave nothing away.

"I do want to learn."

"Then, present your hand."

I threw caution and good sense to the wind as I held out my hand.

"Don't worry," Lord Pinge said. "It's only water."

He placed the single drop on my first knuckle. The droplet ever so slowly slid down my finger until it dangled from my fingertip.

"Just enough water to stay on your finger," he explained. "If—and only if—you do not move. The slightest motion, the slightest quiver, and the drop will fall. Your goal—your task—is to hold the drop there until the water dries."

Sounded easy enough, but like everything at Nocmara, it wasn't. Within a few breaths, the drop fell, splashing on the floor at my feet.

"Damn! I failed," I said.

"So, we try again. Hand up. Don't focus on your hand. Focus on the drop."

It slid down to my fingertip once again. How he knew the exact amount of water to create the effect was a mystery. That, by itself, was impressive, yet the drops fell. I tried again, and again, and again, with no better results. By the end of class, the drops echoed like claps of thunder as they hit the floor announcing yet another failure.

"Well, I'm out of water," Lord Pinge said. "Come back tomorrow and we'll pick up where we left off."

Sun, after mind-numbing sun, the same thing. I longed for the suns when staring at the back of his head was all I had to worry about. I wanted to scream.

On the fifteenth sun, I noticed something new. Inside the glistening drop was a tiny little world where the reflections of light from the window danced within. The distorted image of Lord Pinge floated upside down on the surface. Like a mirror, I could see a faint reflection of myself. All the colors of the world swirled in this tiny drop. My heartbeat created a twitch and the drop fell, yet I couldn't wait for another drop. This discovery was enchanting. With every successive drop, there were new details and colors I'd never seen before.

"We are running out of sunlight," Lord Pinge interrupted. "Come back tomorrow."

"Wait … wait … just one more."

Lord Pinge smiled. He picked up his cup and departed without a word.

On my way to the dining hall, details jumped out at me for the first time—the color of the mortar between the wall-stones, the slight unevenness of the floor, and the spider spinning its web high up in the corner. During the evening meal, I saw my friends with new eyes. Thin strands of blond hair in Flames's overwise red mane stood out like black sheep in a flock of white. Tomas was missing a piece of his pinky nail on this left hand. Tiny flecks of gold dotted Pertwee's brown eyes. The world was amazing and it took me more than thirteen winters to notice.

My impatience with Lord Pinge's task vanished. When I had finished exploring the world within the drop, my attention turned to the air on my face, the hardness of the stones under my feet, and the tiny vibrations of my heartbeat. And then the vibrations stopped.

"I did it. The water is dried up. I did it!"

"Yes. Yes, you did," Lord Pinge said. "That's great. Come back next sun and we'll continue."

"But ... but I did it."

"Yes, you did. With one hand. Next time, we'll use two hands."

He left grinning from ear to ear just when I thought I was getting somewhere.

Two hands were not twice as hard, it was four times more difficult. It felt like I was starting from scratch. When the first drop fell, the second was right behind. My impatience was returning with a vengeance. A moon passed, and then another, and I still couldn't do it.

Battle class felt more like a losing battle and the gobbledygook in my book was not congealing into words. I needed to defeat my inner demons, my impatience. It was holding me back.

You know what? I thought. *Let the drops fall. What difference does it make? They fall. They don't fall. Why was I making such a big deal of it? Frustration won't get me to my goal any quicker. I'll succeed when the time is right.*

And they didn't fall. The drops grew smaller and smaller until they disappeared.

"Nice, Timikia. You finally understand."

"So, what's tomorrow, two hands and a foot?"

"There is no tomorrow for you and me. Lord Mar will summon you and a new class will be assigned. I have enjoyed getting to know you over the last ... what is it, almost two winters? I will miss our silent chats."

Lord Pinge patted my head like a puppy once again and strolled out of my life.

I had done it. I had learned the secret. You do what you need to do. No failure, no success, just moving forward, one sun at a time. It was so simple. How did I not see it before? Time for me to get to work.

The blood-red sunbeams broke over the wall and painted the court in a glimmering golden shine as battle class began. There was no frustration this sun. When I broke position to prevent falling, I started again. Now that every mistake wasn't followed by the self-vitriol of my soul, I stood like a proud flamingo.

"There's been a change in you, fledgling," Lord Vicar said without his usual venom.

"Hopefully a change for the better, my Lord."

"Maybe yes. Maybe no. We'll see."

He spun around to kick my leg out from under me. I leaped over his strike and landed, ever the flamingo. With a second rotation, he targeted my head. I ducked and still stood like the grand pink bird I knew I was.

"Hmmm. Come with me, fledgling."

I followed him out of the court and down the hall. My heart raced, wondering if he was leading me to a secluded room where he could pummel me senseless. After ascending a flight of stairs, we entered a large training court. Ten to twenty fledglings were practicing actual fighting skills. My heart raced, this time with excitement.

"Lord Kanar," Vicar said, motioning to have him join us. "This fledgling has proven he is not totally worthless. I would like to leave him in your capable hands."

Lord Kanar was a tall man with worn hands and face. A deep scar ran from his right eye to the bottom of his jaw. It was the face of a battle-hardened veteran.

"Rest assured, my good Lord," he said, "I will make sure we purge any worthlessness out of this fledgling."

Before Lord Vicar turned to leave, I had one important thing left to say.

"Lord Vicar," my words stopped him in his tracks. "You were wrong. I don't hate you, because I finally understand you. Thank you for everything, my Lord."

With a wink, he vanished down the steps.

Lord Kanar stopped the class and addressed them.

"Boys … we are joined this sun by Timikia. You may not know him yet but take the opportunity to become acquainted. He was mentored by the great Lord Whispa and if you don't know that name, you should. Tell me, Timikia, do you know the six disciplines of necromancer warfare?"

By the powers, was this another trap? Was I supposed to know this or not? Was this another Lord Whispa cheat? Taking my chances, I answered the question truthfully.

"One is wand skills. Two, spells. Three, curses. Four, emotation. Five, minions and, of course, the poison skills."

"Excellent. Since a wand isn't necessary for the other five disciplines, why is it important to practice with one?"

"A wand is not the source of a necromancer's power. That comes from within. A wand is more like a soldier's sword. The other five disciplines are more powerful, but not as fast. They are more like a bow. To use a bow, you have to mount the arrow, draw the string, aim, and release. Similarly, a spell takes time to summon, charge, aim, and release. If you're fighting in close-quarters, you'd be dead before you cast it. A wand can strike four opponents within a breath. I always thought of a wand as the last line of offense or defense."

"Right again, Timikia." Lord Kanar turned to face the fledglings. "Boys, if he knows this much on his first sun here, imagine what else might be in his little head. You should get to know him."

And just like that, I was a celebrity.

"Come," Lord Kanar said as he guided me toward a hefty boy. "This is your sparring partner, Scarper. You know a lot of things, but he knows things you don't, so pay attention. You'll live longer."

"Excuse me, Lord Kanar, may I work with Flames or Zip? They're friends of mine."

"No, you may not. Some of our drills use live magic. You might hold back on a friend, or more precisely, they may hold back on you. That's something we don't allow here."

Fortunately for me, there were no live drills that sun.

Laying on my bed, I reveled in my accomplishments. My friends poured praise on me for joining them in Lord Kanar's class. I couldn't wait to see what would replace my question mark class. Best of all, I had discovered patience. What could make this sun any better? Cracking the code.

After firing up the lamp, I opened the book that I had been trying to read all at once. What if I focused on reading a single word? That's what a patient fledgling would do. You can't see the forest until you see a single tree. The two most common words are "the" and "and." I'll start with those. Scanning for the letter "t," "h," and "e," I quickly found them. The "h" was three symbols from the "t," and the "e" seven. Looking for other occurrences, I found four more in the first ten pages that were three and seven characters apart. I discovered a similar pattern with the word "and." Other cases of the letters, however, were not in the same sequence. Still, it was the first pattern I had noticed. What did the numbers three and seven have in common? They're odd numbers. They're prime numbers. They're every other prime number. If the pattern continued, then the fourth letter in the word would be thirteen characters from the first.

"M" was the first letter in the book. Jumping three letters, was a "y." In the seventh position was an "n." Continuing to the thirteenth letter "a," nineteenth "m," and the twenty-ninth "e." I reviewed the phrase. If I split "MYNAME" after the "y," I have "My name." That would be a good opening for a spell book.

The quill-work of the writer always appeared sloppy. Random spills of ink dotted the page. Not the work of an experienced pen-man, or was it? The penmanship of every fledgling was expected to be impeccable. It would follow that a lord's penmanship would be even better. What if the spots are not by accident, but by design? There's a spot near the "m" and another near the "n." The beginning of a new word perhaps? I found an "i" followed by an "s" at character 43. The fifty-third character was an "L" and it too had a spot just below it. This was followed by "o," "r," and "d." "My name is Lord"—I was about to find out who wrote this book. With tingling fingers, I located a "T" and then the trail went cold. The rest of the letters made no sense.

I stayed up long into the night struggling with the lost patten. I'm so close I can almost taste it. After a certain number of characters, the pattern changed. I heard the footsteps of attendants, as they began knocking on fledglings' doors. I've been at this all night and I only have four words for my efforts. UNLESS—it doubles back on itself. The last character I found was letter eighty-nine. What if the pattern reversed on the ninetieth letter? The letter before the last "T" is an "i." If that were the second prime number, then the following characters going backward would be "m-i-c-u-s. My name is Lord Timicus."

Chapter #12

Last Lesson

Timikia had a new zip to his step as he entered my chambers. He may have learned patience, but modesty still eluded him. These early fledglings think they know so much. They know nothing. He doesn't even understand that when you greet a lord, the lord should speak first.

"You summoned me, Lord Mar?" Timikia said.

"Yes, fledgling, I did. I hear you have made a breakthrough."

"The last few suns have been very productive, my Lord."

"Yes, that is what I understand. Promoted in battle class, cracked your code, and Lord Pinge says you need a new instructor."

"Yes, my Lord. I'm anxious for a new class," said the fledgling, reeking of arrogance.

"I've been giving that some thought. I could send you to potions class or—since you cracked the code— spells training. Which would you prefer?"

"How about both?" asked Timikia.

"There is only time for three classes in a sun."

"I could give up reading class."

"Then when are you going to translate your book? Spell class is useless without the book."

"I can read the book after my classes."

"At night? That won't leave much time for sleep."

"I assure you, my Lord, I can handle it."

My first reaction was to say no—but this could be a good test of his breaking point.

"All right then, two classes it is. Report to Lord Japisan's spell class second period. Third period, report to Guardian Merse's potions group. Now, runoff. I'm busy."

The sound of Timikia's footsteps disappeared down the hall. Heavy boots stepped out from the curtain behind me.

"I told you," said Lord Loter. "He doesn't understand."

"Maybe not. Time will tell."

"If we're not careful, he could end up being just like his father."

"That could be a good thing. Don't worry. I'll personally keep an eye on him. You have to admit, he does have the spark."

"So did his father and we know how that turned out." Lord Loter turned toward the door.

He departed with a stern look, leaving me with my thoughts. *He was right. Timikia was a bull among the sheep. The Brotherhood doesn't need a bull, we need a ram. If we're going to survive, we need more leaders, not another reckless egomaniac. If we can guide Timikia ... that would be good ... but if we can't ...*

***

I sat in the arena's balcony as the sun rose watching the fledglings. Paired with an older, bigger, and more experienced boy, Timikia was holding this own. After a mere moon, his wand skills were quite advanced. Maybe too advanced. Everyone cheered him on as he beat two heavily favored fledglings in live combat. At this rate of progress, he could move into level three battle class in a few more moons. Another record.

As the class began wrapping up, I proceeded down the steps and stood by the door. The boys filed out as I waited for him.

"Timikia!"

Stunned, he stopped cold and slowly turned to face me.

"May I have a word with you?"

"Good sun, Lord Mar. It's not often I see you in this part of the school. Is there something you wish of me?"

"Yes, young fledgling. I noticed your wand skills are quite good for someone with so little experience. No one can seem to parry you and your attacks are spot on. Your evasion skills are quite developed. You destroyed that older boy and he's been in this class for two winters. Care to explain how that can be?"

"Umm ... I, ah ..."

"The worst thing you could do at this moment is lie to me."

"It was a game I played with Lord Whispa as a child."

"Please explain this—game."

"We used to paint. Lord Whispa would have me hold my paintbrush out with my arm fully extended. Then, using just my fingers, he would have me paint small, perfect circles. Sometimes he would try and slap my hand away. I learned to see him coming and avoid him. It was fun. It made me laugh. We played often and for long stretches at a time."

"I see. Were there any games that are helping you in potions class? I've heard you made a first-rate healing potion on only your third sun there."

"Yes …"

"Go on."

"We would make pastries in the kitchen. He'd never let me use measuring tins. I always had to feel the weight of the sugar and flour. I had to guess the amount of oil as I poured it. Sometimes the desserts were a disaster and we would laugh. We laughed a lot."

"So, you became an expert at measuring powders and fluids by hand?"

"Yeah … but I can't unlearn what I already know. Are you going to kick me out?"

"No. What Lord Whispa taught you were skills, not lessons. A lesson guides your life. Anyone can master a skill with enough time. You learned when you were just a little boy, that's all. The lesson here is not to let it go to your head. I've noticed that you receive much attention from the other boys. That sort of thing can mess with a young necromancer's mind. Makes you think you're special. You're just the same as they are. You just started earlier. If you remember any other—games—I want you to report them to me. Do you understand?"

As the moons passed, Timikia came to me with descriptions of games, stories, and playtime he shared with Lord Whispa. I have to admit, Lord Whispa was clever. Nothing noticeable to others at the time, but he clearly had a plan.

Timikia breezed through class after class. By the time he was fifteen winters, two of the nine Council Lords had cleared him to be promoted to guardian. A few moons later, two more gave him the nod. Shortly before his sixteenth anniversary, the only two holdouts were Lord Loter and myself.

"You can't be serious," said Lord Loter. "You can't unleash a sixteen-winter-old guardian on the world. He's not ready!"

"He's passed every class, every challenge, with flying colors. There is no justification to hold him back."

"HE'S FLIPPING SIXTEEN! His father was eighteen and that

used to be the record. And we all know the mistakes he made. Timikia walks around this school like he owns the place. That's a lesson he hasn't learned. Really—REALLY—you want to promote that punk?"

"Rumors of his abilities have already leaked beyond these walls. It would be politically difficult to explain not promoting him."

Lord Loter balled up his fists, seething with frustration.

"No, no, no—mark my words, he'll run after the first demon he sees, one he's not ready for, and he'll be dead!"

"Then what do you suggest when the kings come to hire him, asking for him by name?"

"Let me confront him one last time. Maybe I can beat some sense into him before it's too late."

I didn't like the sound of that, but I was running out of options.

"I'll ask him to meet me in the battle arena tomorrow night, just after dusk," I began. "It will be deserted by then. Most of the school will be dining. You can confront him there."

Chapter #13

Battle Class

"**L**et's start with Herc versus Timikia," said Lord Kanar.

Damn, I had to be first. Herc's height gave him a major reach advantage. I remembered the words of Lord Whispa, "Never move your shoulder when you can move your elbow. Never move your elbow when you can twist your wrist. Never twist your wrist when you can angle your fingers. Smaller is always the better way. It's not about power, it's about angles."

"Yeah, whoop'em, Herc," cried a boy in the crowd. "Smoke the new kid. Herc, Herc, Herc, Herc" came the chant.

Clearly, the crowd was on his side. He looked pretty confident. If I was him, I would have been too.

"He likes to blind you by going for the head," Flames whispered. "Remember to duck."

Wise words from someone who had been here a while and probably took a few blows to the head himself. It was a good tip. Lord Whispa had always said, "Know your enemy."

"Timikia," Lord Kanar began, "I know this is your first live spar, so keep in mind we're not trying to hurt each other."

"Yeah," Herc spat, "as if he's going to hit me."

"Do you mind if I finish, FLEDGLING HERC?"

"Sorry, my Lord."

"No long holds," Lord Kanar continued. "Only quick touches. We're going for points, not injuries. All right fledglings, first to three. Ready? Battle!"

I held my wand out in front to keep Herc at bay. His toothy grin was nerve-racking. He kept his left hand behind his back. I wasn't sure why, but I imitated his actions anyway. The back left hand worked as a counterweight and improved my balance. The best tips are learned from superior opponents.

No, you don't, I thought as Herc's strike whizzed over my head. *You're going to have to do better than that. Thanks, Flames, I owe you one.*

Herc tried to circle me, but I was too smart for that. I might have been new, but wasn't falling for simple strategies.

Another strike to the head? I thought. *Really? That's the best you've got? Come on, try that one more time.*

He lunged for my head once again. Instead of ducking, I deflected his wand with mine. Sparks flew the moment our wands touched. With a quick angle change, I struck him in the elbow. He flinched and dropped his wand to the sand.

"HALT!" Lord Kanar said. "Timikia one. Herc nothing."

"YEAH!" Flames erupted. "Two more. Two more!"

At least I have one fan, and then Zip joined in. All right, two fans. Lord Kanar motioned us back to our starting positions.

"Ready! BATTLE!"

Your grin isn't so big now, is it, big boy? I thought. *More circles? It didn't work before, what makes him think it will work now? Another headshot? This guy's a one-trick pony. Again, to the head—WHAT! Ahhh—damn my knee. It's not pain. It's not pain. Oh yeah, it's pain.*

"Herc! Herc! Herc! Herc!" the boys' voices grew louder.

"Can you stand?" Lord Kanar asked.

Get up, Timikia, I said to myself. *Don't let the others see your weakness. GET UP!*

"The tendon behind the knee is a painful spot," Lord Kanar said. "Timikia, are you sure you wish to continue?"

"Yeah."

I'll give you that one, Herc, my mind raced, *but no more. No more!*

"BATTLE!"

There's that grin again, my mind continued. *Come on, try that double move one more time. Duck low. Block the body shot. Slide and cut to the hip.*

Herc flinched, clutching his side.

"Tim-i-kia! Tim-i-kia! Tim-i-kia!" Flames and Zip chanted on and on.

A third boy joined in, and then another, and another. By the time we returned to our starting positions, three-quarters of the class was chanting my name.

"Two to one, Timikia. Ready! BATTLE!"

Where's the big grin now, huh? What hurts more, my wand or the fact you're losing to a newbie? Now what? He's already seen my best. I doubt I'll fool him with that again.

His attacks were getting better every time. I was getting nervous. Then I thought, *I don't have to stop his wand, just his arm.*

On his next attack, I grabbed his wrist and slid my wand up his tricep to the armpit.

"YEAH!" Flames screamed.

The crowd went crazy.

"ALL RIGHT, ALL RIGHT, ALL RIGHT, BOYS! CALM DOWN!" Lord Kanar demanded. "Return to your seats. Timikia— that last strike was unnecessarily long. Be more careful in the future or I'll match you up with me next time."

"Sorry, my Lord. It was an accident. It won't happen again. Sorry, Herc. Good match."

He gave me a quick nod while shaking his arm awake. I hoped that meant we're good. I had enough enemies.

Patting me on the back, Flames whispered, "That's Herc's first loss in three moons."

Later that sun, I won another match, three to two. I was popular again. As the class ended, a group of boys surrounded me. We all strolled out of the court together before being stopped by a single voice.

"Timikia!"

What was he doing here? I thought.

"May I have a word with you?" Lord Mar said.

His seriousness struck fear in my heart. The other boys fled like a flock of birds avoiding a hawk, leaving the two of us alone in the hallway.

Now what? I thought.

"Good sun, Lord Mar. It's not often we see you in this part of the school. Is there something you wish of me?"

"Yes, there is, young fledgling. I noticed …"

I had fallen into another trap. It's like they don't want me to succeed. This was so frustrating.

"The worst thing you could do at this moment is lie to me," Lord Mar said in a deadly serious tone.

He looked as if he was trying to peer into my soul. If the truth would get me kicked out, why shouldn't I lie? Lying would be the easy way. But I was never a good liar. If I get kicked out, at least I'd leave with my head held high.

"We used to paint. Lord Whispa would—"

With every word, I expected him to interrupt and boot me out. But the truth was liberating. I hadn't felt so free since arriving at these gray walls. Then, he asked about my cheats for the potions class. With everything to lose, but my self-respect, I continued.

"So, you became an expert at measuring powders by hand?" Lord Mar said.

This is so unfair. I came to Nocmara knowing how to read four languages. Was that a cheat too? I'm a crack archer and an excellent horseman. Are those cheats? Was I supposed to spend the first twelve winters of my life sitting in the corner, staring at the walls?

"Yeah ... but I can't unlearn what I already know. Are you going to kick me out?"

"No. What Lord Whispa taught you were skills, not lessons ..."

Then he said some other words that jumbled in my head. Something about skills and lessons—I don't know. All I heard was I get to stay. I had faced so many trials, pains, and abuse since coming here, but keeping Lord Whispa's secrets was the hardest task of all.

"If you remember any other—games—I want you to report them to me. Do you understand?"

After he was out of sight, I sat down on the cold floor hanging my head in disbelief. Then, I had an epiphany. I wanted to be a lord SO BAD! Therein lies the problem. The fear of having my dream stripped away was crushing my soul. From now on I will fight. I will strive. I will work harder than any other fledgling, but—I am not defined by being a lord. I don't have to be a lord to be happy or successful. It's what I want, but I may not get it and I don't need it. This truth set me free. No more hiding Lord Whispa's secrets. No more holding back. I am Timikia, son of Lord Timicus. No one can take that away from me, not even the Council of Nine. They want to see what I can do? Get out of my way, Nocmara. Watch me rise!

***

"WHOA!" Lord Kanar shouted, "Timikia! What in the name of the other side are you doing?"

"Sparring, my Lord. I was about to attack with a double twist thrust."

Why did he stop us in midpoint? In my three moons of live combat, he's never done that.

"You're emoting."

The pale blue haze in front of my eyes came into focus. I really was emoting.

"What's wrong with that?" I asked.

"What's wrong with that? We don't use emotation in class. It's too dangerous."

"Guardian Pecta, take Timikia to the ready room and determine the extent of his abilities and what level of control he has over them," said Lord Kanar, and then he faced me again.

"Timikia, until you can control your emotation, or better yet, turn it off, you are banned from live combat practice."

The crowd grew quiet. In a breath, they had gone from cheering me to fearing me, as I followed the guardian to a secluded room.

"Damn," Guardian Pecta said, "you're emoting already. Aren't you only sixteen winters?"

"Yeah. Just barely."

"I was seventeen before I could emote. Eighteen before I could control it."

"How old are you now?" I asked.

"Twenty-five."

"When were you promoted to guardian?"

"Last winter. But enough about me. Emote for me."

"I ... I don't know how."

"What do you mean you don't know how? I just saw you do it."

"Yeah ... and I've done it a couple of times before. It just ... sort of happens."

"Wow, that's dangerous. Emotation is caused by powerful emotions, hence the name. What happened out there in the ring? Describe it to me," said Guardian Pecta.

"Let's see. I was up two nothing and then Flames scored two points in a row."

"And you got mad."

"Yeah, I guess I did. That's bad, right? Lord Kanar tells us to stay calm."

"That's true. Being in control helps with spells and curses as well. However, to emote you need to let go. That's where the control part comes in. You need to go from calm to extreme and back on demand."

"So, it's all about anger?" I asked.

"No, not necessarily. Any emotion will do. Hate, pain, fear …
love, it's any emotion that makes your skin tingle. Give it a try. Think
back. Picture the scene. Think back to a skin-tingling moment. Be
there. Feel every feeling. Smell every scent. Hear every sound. Be
there."

Loter's face rose up in front of me—that arrogant, smug, grimy
face. That's it—Loter called me a "bastard child of a whore" one time
too many! My body stiffened. The world turned blue. The blue smoke
streamed everywhere. Powerful and alive, I felt like I could take on
hell itself. Through the blue fog, I saw Guardian Pecta lying still
against the wall. The fog disbursed as panic replaced my anger, I
helped the stunned guardian to his feet.

"Are you all right?" I asked.

"I don't know what you were thinking—but damn. You blew me
halfway across the room. You're going to have to work hard to control
that kind of power."

It was three moons before Lord Kanar allowed me back into the
ring. Three moons of dealing with my repressed rage. Understanding
the source of my most intense emotions allowed me to find greater
peace. I slept better. I was happier. My wand skills improved. After
defeating every other fledgling in the class without a loss, I joined
Pertwee in the top battle group.

Chapter #14

Minions

"Timikia, what are you doing here?" said Zip.

"I graduated out of potions class last sun."

"WHAT? I know potions is one of the easier classes, but it took me a winter and a half. What's it been for you? About four moons?"

"Three. What do you have to do to bust out of *this* place?"

"Four skels at once or two skels and a golem."

"How are you doing?" I asked.

"Two boneheads so far. I haven't seen the other side yet. It's a lot harder than it seems."

"I know you can do it, Zip. Keep at it. How do I get started?"

"Report to Lord Kestel and he'll get you going."

He was the oldest lord I had ever met. Bald on top and scruffy on the chin. An odd odor filled the air as I approached him. He was missing an eye. No patch, just folded skin over a dark hole.

"Timikia! I've been expecting you."

"Very appreciative to be here, my Lord."

"Normally, you'd start by raising chipmunks or something similar. But in your case, fame proceeds you. I've heard you've already seen the other side."

"Just once, my Lord, and that was under dubious circumstances."

"Yes … I've heard the story. Lord Loter can definitely get under one's skin. The first time you punch through the wall is the hardest. And you've already done that. What do you say we skip chipmunks and go right to the fun stuff?"

"If you think I'm ready, my Lord."

He led me to a small, dimly lit room. I sat cross-legged on the floor as he instructed.

"Pain helps," Lord Kestel said. "Take out your wand."

Scowling at the sight of such a limited wand, he continued his instructions.

"You're never going to get enough pain out of that wand—at least holding it like that. Hold it by the head instead."

"Ummm … I thought wands didn't like that." I said.

"Oh, they don't. That's why it works. It will take you some time, maybe as long as eight winters to see past the barrier. But I have a feeling you'll do it faster. Do you know the three tenets of seeing the other side?"

"Feed off of spirit energy. Increase the reach of minion control. And … find warrior spirits for your golems—"

"Golems? As in more than one? Aren't you ambitious?" said Lord Kestel.

"My mentor, Lord Whispa, had three. So did my father."

"Yes, but both of them were anomalies. Lord Whispa could also hold two wands at once. Just focus on getting one really good golem spirit. One great golem is worth three average ones. You have to be careful about selecting spirits for your golem. Many dead souls would say or do anything to return to this world. Anything. They can weave an excellent story that will come crashing down during your first battle. Choose well. I'll leave you to practice."

As he closed the door, a sliver of light crept in from underneath. The only sounds came from my breath and the steady beat of my heart.

"I'm sorry, my friend. I know you're going to hate this," I spoke to my wand.

Sparks shot up my spine as I clutched the lizard skull. It was like being back in the room all over again. I could see his little face growling at me in my mind. About three hundred breaths in, a gray fog crept into the room. The walls seemed to melt away, and the floor vanished below my legs. And then the wisps. Some had faint outlines of faces. Others were more like waves in the sea. I floated among them like a jellyfish in an ocean of eels. So many. There were so many. The faint sound of buzzing grew louder, like honey bees near the hive. The buzz transformed into whispers, the whispers of thousands. The whispers became voices. So many voices that it was deafening. I instinctively covered my ears. My wand took that chance to exact its vengeance. Agony lit up my skull. The pain shot around my head and settled behind my eyes. My focus was diverted from the thundering voices as

I struggled to control the pain.

A single wisp emerged from the swell. I could sense its determination to communicate.

"Do ya cag adavi a ..."

It was a blur of meaningless sounds when I jammed my wand into my chest. My ribs felt like they were exploding. *Bare the pain*, I thought. *Use the pain.*

"What do you want?" I screamed.

"Do you si pisa meteal ... Do you know oop situa ... Do you know who I am?"

"NO!"

"Yes, you agisa metaia oo uis ... prized boy."

Prized boy? Only he called me that. He was the only one who ever called me that.

"Lord Whispa?" I questioned.

"Yes, Timikia. Focus sip era verbe ... focus auy be gea be ... focus on the sound of my voice. Drop the wand."

As it fell to the floor, the pain subsided except for a throbbing in my fingers. Everything went dark. I floated in empty space face to face with my mentor, Lord Whispa's spirit.

"Are you really my Lord Whispa?"

"Yes."

His words wailed like far-off echoes.

"I have been patiently awaiting your arrival. You are younger than I would have imagined."

"Is this the other side?"

"No. You pulled my spirit to the in-between. The quiet between the living and the dead. Here we can talk. You will not be able to hold me here for long. So, ask your questions quickly."

"Why did you cheat for me?"

"The Brotherhood doesn't know everything. It just thinks it does. I was proving there was a better way to train necromancers. Train them faster. Increase their survival rate."

"You almost got me kicked out of Nocmara."

"And yet, here you are. A fledgling that sees."

"On my first try, no less. So, I was your lab chipmunk. Nothing more than an experiment—another spell, another curse, another trick."

"No, Timikia. I couldn't have loved you more if you were my own son."

"Then why? Why chance cheating?"

"They call it cheating. Timikia, you might be the new breed of necromancer. The Brotherhood is dying. Unless something changes, it won't survive. You might be the beginning of that something."

His wisp jerked as if tugged from behind.

"I'm being pulled back," he said. "I don't have much time. What else do you want to know?"

"Is my father with you?"

"I have searched for him to no avail. There are millions of souls here. I fear I may never find him."

"I need a great warrior for my golem. Can you help find one?"

"Yes … si beere pa de bali …"

I sat alone in the dark as his wisp faded.

Chapter #15

The Confrontation

It started as a small purple globe floating between my hands. I tried to stretch it, but it wouldn't bend to my will. It morphed into a silvery disc. Rolling my hands, I began to make it spin. AHHH!

"FLAMES! You idiot. What's wrong with you? You scared the crap out of me."

"Sorry, guy," he laughed. "It's just time to get ready for Pertwee's promotion ceremony. This is a big sun, Timikia. The first of our little group to make guardian. We don't want to be late."

"When you're right, you're right. But couldn't you just say hello and not grab me from behind?"

"Yeah, but what's the fun in that. What were you working on? It looked interesting."

"Oh … just some spell in my father's book. He called it the death wall. It was the last spell he was working on before he died."

"What does it do? I've never seen anything like it," said Flames.

"It brings up the barrier between our world and the other side. Then, theoretically, you can sweep it around the battlefield and it sucks up everything in its path."

"WHOA! That sounds amazing!"

"It would be, but he never got it to work. I think his attack tangent is way off. He tried to pull it from the other side. I think you have to scrape it off instead. I don't know. I can't get it to work either."

"That's too bad. Hey, have you heard the rumors about who they picked for Pertwee's show battle?"

"No, I can't say I have," I said.

I was lying. Show battles were a big deal. One last cross of wands before the new guardian heads out the door. It's an honor to be selected as the new guardian's opponent. It's usually saved for a fledgling getting close to promotion himself. Keeping the secret was all part of the fun.

"Odds on favorite it's going to Herc," Flames said. "Whoever they pick, Pertwee is going to mop the floor with him."

"We'll see," I said. "You never know."

"Oh, before I forget, an attendant gave me this note for you."

After breaking the seal, I read the message.

"This is odd. Lord Mar wants me to meet him in the battle training court after dinner. I wonder what he wants. Strange place to meet."

"Maybe he wants to show you one of his personal attacks. Ah, whatever it is, don't worry about it. Come on, grab your stuff, and let's go. I want to get a good seat."

Zip, Flames, Tomas, and I climbed up to the viewing deck of the arena. Everyone was there. It's not every sun a fledgling gets promoted to guardian. Pertwee had made quite a name for himself in the last winter. Everyone in my group of friends was proud of him.

A hush fell over the crowd as Lord Hocner stepped into the arena.

"For the last twenty-five winters," Lord Hocner began. "I have had the duty—no privilege—of presiding over a fledgling's promotion to guardian. And this sun will be no exception. Pertwee has been a model fledgling and has passed every class with flying colors. He has distinguished himself as being the first fledgling in ten winters to raise and control an iron golem and three skeletons simultaneously."

The crowd cheered. Lord Hocner, ever the showman, waited for them to quiet down.

"He has mastered every curse known to the Brotherhood."

That drew another explosion from the audience. As always, Lord Hocner awaited silence.

"So, not to bore you any further with my blow-heartedness—"

Laughter rang out.

"Please raise your voices for Nocmara's senior fledgling—Pertwee!"

Massive hoots and hollers erupted as Pertwee stepped into the arena. His new green armor sparkled in the sunlight. The gold necromancer emblem on this chest glinted like a gemstone. His face was glowing even brighter than his armor. As he walked to the center ring, we all stood for his triumph. The chants roared on until Lord Hocner raised his hands to hush the crowd.

"Do you Pertwee," Lord Hocner began, "swear your undying allegiance to the Brotherhood, its Council, and all its objectives?"

"I do."

"Do you Pertwee, promise to accept all and any assignments the Brotherhood may bestow on you, to protect and promote its kings—and queen—and kingdoms, and personally safeguard the Southern Realm from all entities internal and external?"

"I do."

"Do you Pertwee promise to strive with all your earthly abilities to become a lord, complete the poisoning, and uphold all the traditions, honor, and image of the Brotherhood?"

"I do."

"Then with that, attendants, fledglings, guardians, and lords, I present to you the Brotherhood's newest guardian—Guardian Pertwee!"

The cheers were deafening, echoing around the arena like thunder.

"And now the moment I'm sure you've all been waiting for—the announcement of who Lord Mar has selected for Pertwee's first battle as a guardian ..."

What a ham. He just had to draw out the suspense.

"Timikia, would you please join us in the ring."

My friends were shocked. A chuckling Pertwee shook his head. The crowd chanted my name as I descended the stairs and took my place in the circle.

"Why did it have to be you?" Pertwee whispered in my ear. "You and that little wand of yours are a pain in the ass."

"QUIET EVERYONE!" Lord Hocner said. "I have a surprise announcement. For the first time in a show battle, Lord Mar has authorized the use of emotation."

A stunned muffle filtered through the arena. Pertwee and I exchanged concerned looks.

"What the hell?" mouthed Pertwee.

"And—instead of three points, this battle will be to five points."

This drew another round of murmurs.

"Lord Mar has commanded that neither combatant shall hold back and that each of you emote at least three times during the match. The contest will continue until you do. Please take your positions."

The crowd was eerily silent, so much so that I could hear the sand squishing under my boots.

"Combatants ready? Fight!"

Pertwee had amazing footwork. He could rush in, strike and

retreat faster than any fledgling in the school. Ever since Lord Mar told me I had been selected, I planned to let him win. I wanted him to enjoy this exciting sun. But five points with emotations? That's a different story. Under these conditions, one, or both of us, may not walk off under his own power.

He lunged in for a low strike. Narrowly avoiding it, I deftly side-stepped, but my movement left me off balance. Pertwee spun and struck me in the back. It didn't hurt much. It was a good clean touch. It's what I'd come to expect of him. I gave him a nod of acknowledgment. Now, it was my turn. Let's see if he can stop this one. Faint left, evade right, faint low, roll, and cut to the forearm.

Pertwee snickered as he rubbed his arm. "Not bad, Timikia," he added. "Not bad at all."

"I don't see any emotion from either of you," said Lord Hocner. "Remember you're out there until you do."

Pertwee stepped to the right. His eyes began to glow and his head lit up in a blue fireball. With a swirl of his arms, he sent an energy blast straight at me. I dove to the dirt as the beam whizzed over my head. The attack was really slow. A first winter's fledgling could have dodged that. He had missed on purpose.

"HALT!" Lord Hocner shouted. "What was that? My grandmother could emote better than that and she's dead. Pertwee—I said no holding back. That one doesn't count toward your three. This is your show battle, try putting on a show. Let's try that again, shall we?"

Pertwee's lips uttered, "I'm sorry."

"Ready? Battle!"

He bull rushed me, wand extended. I leapt over the low attack and turned to see him emoting. I pictured Loter's face. By the powers I hated that man, and his disgusting image always charged me up. We blasted out simultaneously. The concussion of the colliding energy blew us both across the arena. Ugh—piercing pain came from my knee. Pertwee was clutching his back, stumbling to get to his feet. I lay in the sand, panting.

"That was good," Lord Hocner commented. "I will award each of you one point. Assume your positions."

"No!" I spat. "I'm done. This isn't a show. You're setting up a blood-bath."

"Timikia, assume your position!" Lord Hocner barked.

"Not a chance. I'm not going to injure my friend or burden him with the guilt of injuring me for you, the crowd, or this whole damn school."

I limped my way toward the doors.

"Timikia, STOP!" Lord Hocner shouted.

"You want to see emotation? Watch this!"

Over four winters of rage rose inside me. Half my mana rose off my shoulders. Turning, I blew the doors open sending one of them flying off its hinges. Stomping out of the arena, I found myself amid the celebration dinner. The attendants who were still setting up, were white with panic. Food flew as I flipped a table and stormed back to my room.

I sat in my room seething as I waited for Nocmara to react. Shortly before dusk, there came a wrap at my door.

"Come in."

"You all right, guy?"

"Flames, Zip, Tomus … thank you for coming. I needed to see friendly faces right now. How mad is Pertwee? I completely screwed up his show battle."

"Mad?" Flames said. "He's not mad. At least not at you. He bolted right after you left. No one has seen him since. He's probably hiding out somewhere. I can't imagine what's going through his head."

"Are the guards coming for me? To throw me out the doors, into the dungeon or someplace worse?"

"I don't know. There's a lot of whispering going on. Let's just say you're going to be everyone's dinner-party story for a long time."

My friends hugged me for a few moments.

"I know Nocmara doesn't like rule-breakers," Zip said, "but they would be fools to bounce you out of here. Your emote was two arm lengths over your head. You'd be one hell of a lord. You'd get your portrait on the wall for sure. Probably right next to your father's."

"Thanks, Zip. I just want you guys to know—if I never see you again after tonight—how much I have appreciated your friendship. This is a crazy place, but you've made it bearable. I have to go meet with Lord Mar. I'm not sure why he messaged me earlier, but I'll bet it's going to be a different conversation now."

We hugged one more time and I left with their sad faces etched in my mind.

"I'm here," I shouted as I entered the battleground. "Lord Mar, are you here?"

Scanning the space, I spotted a dark-hooded figure walking toward me.

"Before you say anything, I know I screwed up. A big-time screw up! But I ..."

Pulling his hood back, it wasn't Lord Mar.

"Loter!"

"LOTER!" he barked.

In a breath, he emoted and blew me off my feet.

"How dare you not address me as 'LORD'! You pathetic little child. I should squash you like a beetle."

I crawled away from him.

"WHY DO YOU HATE ME SO MUCH?"

"You? Hate you? What could possess me to waste a valuable emotion like hate on you? You make me laugh, boy!"

"Then all this is because you hated my father?"

"Where did you get the stupid idea that I hated your father?"

"Lord Whispa told me about the fights you two had."

"Oh sure, we had a few spats, but I admired your father. He was one of the best of us. He was working on spells no lord had dreamt of before. I didn't hate your father. I hated what he did."

"What? What is this big horrible thing he did?"

"HE THREW HIS LIFE AWAY! All that potential was gone because he chose to go head-to-head with a bug. He could have advanced the power of the Brotherhood threefold and he THREW IT ALL AWAY! And for what? A woman."

"That woman is my mother."

"Yeah, not even royal blood, just some scullery maid. He could have found ten just like her in any village in his kingdom."

"You shut up. You don't talk about my mother like that."

"Yeah, look at you. Just like your father. Tears streaming down your face. You can't control your emotions either. Love. That's what did him in. Because of love, he threw his life away for a whore."

"YOU SHUT UP!"

Screaming, I raised the purple death wall for the first time. It exploded from the ground and divided the court in half. I couldn't believe how much mana it took. With what little magic remained in me, I pushed the wall towards Loter. In a panic, he leapt up onto the stone perimeter. The walls of the court shook like a trebuchet strike as the purple barrier pounded into it. Loter struggled to keep his footing. As the death wall dissipated, Loter leapt down to the sandy floor. A demon spirit head rose from his hand as he charged his powerful spell.

"You're completely out of mana now, boy. Look at you. You can't even stand. I could finish you off with one spell."

"Then do it!"

"Don't be like your father. Don't be so anxious for the other side. Don't waste your life, boy. Change the Brotherhood. Change the world."

A herd of footsteps approached from down the hall. Loter retreated out the rear doors before anyone arrived. Led by Pertwee, a mass of students crashed into the court. Pertwee tried to help me to my feet, but I passed out in his arms.

***

I awoke in the healer's room. It hurt to breathe. Lord Mar sat alone next to my cot.

"You mind telling me what happened last night?" he asked.

"Why don't you ask Loter?"

"That's Lord Loter to you, fledgling. I did ask him. He said everything was fine and refused to comment further. I need you to explain something to me. How does a fledgling get into a battle with one of the most dangerous duelers in the Brotherhood and survive?"

"Ask Loter."

"What is to become of you, Timikia?"

"So ... am I done? Has my time at Nocmara come to an end? Time for me to go home?"

"Yes, it's time for you to go. Surrender your wand."

Goodbye, old friend, I thought as I handed the box to Lord Mar.

"You definitely won't be needing this anymore. After all, this is a training wand. Not a proper wand for a guardian."

Pulling an ornate, gold-inlaid box from his robe, he presented it to me. It seemed oddly familiar.

"What's this?" I asked.

"A wand worthy of a guardian."

"You're promoting me?"

"Yes. Lord Loter voted for you this morning. Far be it of me to be the lone holdout."

He gestured to my right. On the cot lay a guardian's suit of armor, shiny and new. A wave of emotions flooded me. I opened the wand box. It held a twisted shaft with a monkey's skull. My father's wand. I only saw it once before, but I would never forget that sun.

"Lord Whispa always wanted you to have it," Lord Mar said. "Many a lord coveted it after your father's demise. I promised Lord

Whispa, on his deathbed, that I would save it for you. You can head home as soon as you're up to it."

"What? No celebration? No show-battle?"

"You fought a lord and lived to tell the tale. I think you've shown off enough. Plus, with the mess you made last sun, I'm afraid you'd destroy the place. They're still fixing the door and I don't know WHAT you and Lord Loter did to the court. What a mess! Rest up. Say goodbye to your friends. Return to the palace and await the assignment the Council has planned for you—Guardian Timikia."

"I just have one more question," I said.

"Of course. What do you wish to know?"

"What was your involvement in last sun's odd events?"

Mar's jaw stiffened. For ten breaths our eyes locked in silence. Neither of us dared blink. He stood and walked out.

Chapter #16

The Price of Alliance

"My dear High Mage Fardarius," I began, "I'm trying to understand your perspective, but clearly there has to be another way."

"No, my good Queen Lika, there isn't."

She relished in flashing the four gold stripes on the arm of her black bodysuit with each demand as if that would somehow intimidate me. Her display of rank did not impress me in any way. When the council asked me to negotiate this alliance, they should have warned me how stubborn Sorceri can be.

"But seriously, a royal pairing? We both need this alliance to counter the growing threat. You know that. I know that. What I don't understand is why a pairing has to be connected to it?"

"There is deep hatred and mistrust between the necros and my kind," High Mage Fararius countered.

"That's necromancers."

"Necros, necromancers, two halves of the same egg. My point is I need probable cause to get the High Coven to agree to such an arrangement. Kinship is always a good persuader."

"But you have seven daughters. I only have one son."

"Yes, Prince Timikia. A daughter of mine should be paired with a lord, but she's one of my lesser daughters. Only a level five after four winters. I can spare this one."

"Don't do us any favors," I said in disgust. "It doesn't matter anyway. Prince Timikia is currently at Nocmara, studying to be a guardian. It could be winters before his return."

"I hear he has already been promoted to guardian," she retorted.

As if the High Mage had planned it, there was a knock at my chamber doors.

"Come."

"I beg your pardon, Queen Lika," Soronto said, "an urgent message has arrived from Nocmara. I thought you might want to read it forthright."

I broke the seal. Fardarius's theory was confirmed.

"This message was written three suns ago. How did you know about my son?" I questioned in disgust.

"We have our ways."

"You mean you have your spies."

"As do you, my Queen. As do you."

"I will discuss this with my son and see if he would be willing."

"Permission? You're going to ask for his permission? He's a Prince. It's his duty. No permission is necessary. Just order him."

"Maybe that's how it works for the Sorceri, but things are different here."

Fardarius rolled her eyes and said, "I will delay my departure a couple of suns to give you time to get his—permission. I suggest you be convincing. Time is not on our side."

As she left my chambers, the gong announcing Timikia's return sounded almost right on cue.

I understood why the Council picked me for this task. The Sorceri are not fond of men and hate necromancers. I am the only Queen of a necromancer kingdom. Plus, given my considerable negotiation skills, it made me the obvious choice. But I was being forced into too many compromises. I didn't expect my son to be a negotiation coin. I didn't trust the High Coven.

"Soronto, please join me!"

"Yes, my Lady. What is your bidding?"

"Guardian Timikia will be—"

"Guardian?"

"Yes. It appears he has been promoted."

"His not even quite seventeen winters yet?"

"I know. Amazing, right? Run down to the kitchen and have them whip up something special. Portal travel always makes Timikia hungry. Tell the royal attendants to prepare the Prince's room and draw a bath. It's been four winters since we've seen him. I want his first sun here to be special. At least as special as it can be on such short notice."

"Right away, my Lady."

Soronto rushed off with a renewed spring in her step. She had a soft spot in her heart for Timikia since the sun he was born.

After finishing up a few land deeds, I strolled down to the front gate anticipating my son's arrival. It was hard being without him. He was my cheer—my happiness. He never left my thoughts. I wondered how becoming a guardian had changed him.

A lone figure in green emerged on the path. Timikia was clad in his new armor. It was no surprise to see him walking as he had always hated the trolley. But no guards? He's a guardian now and he doesn't need them anymore.

"Good sun, Mother," Timikia said.

That was a hug I will never forget.

"Look at you. All shiny and green. Lord Mar must be so proud of you."

"Yeah ... I guess."

"Are you hungry? I have our chef making up something special right now."

"I could eat. You can catch me up on the state of the kingdom on the way. How are things here?"

"Oh, we have our good suns and bad."

"Mother, you were never good at hiding problems from me. What's up?"

"Nothing you need to worry about right now. Let's go have a nice meal."

He stopped in his tracks, staring at me with an old soul's gaze.

"There is no better time than the present. What is happening?"

I was hoping to share a moment of celebration before royal burdens fell upon him.

"I'm working on an alliance with the Sorceri."

"Things have gotten that bad with the Barbarians that you would risk an alliance with the SORCERI?"

"I wish it was the Barbarians. They pulled away from the border about a winter ago. Leaving it totally undefended. They have bigger problems."

"Did the Druids finally invade from the north?"

"Your information is out of date. The Barbarian-Druid clash is old news. They're fighting the Demons now."

"Demons!"

"Yes. Our spies reported that they've been attacked by four tribes. Rumor has it that a third of their lands are under Demon control already."

"That's not good. So, you think they're going to come out of the trench after us next?"

"General Jaker's forces have ambushed a few goblin patrols. The problem is those foul little beasts kill themselves before they can be interrogated. It's a big border. If the demons are scouting for weaknesses, they're going to find them."

"What steps have you taken to secure the area?"

"I moved four legions down there. The Brotherhood has stationed two hundred necromancers at Fort Herridon."

"Two hundred lords?"

"No. A handful of lords. Maybe ten. The rest are guardians. The cost of this is putting a strain on our coffers."

"The Brotherhood isn't funding this themselves? I would think they'd take this threat more seriously."

"You would think, but no. We need this alliance—and soon."

"What can I do to help?" he inquired.

"Funny—you should ask. The Sorceri are demanding a royal pairing as part of the treaty. It's their tradition."

"Wow! What poor sap did you con into that?"

"Funny—you should ask. Unfortunately, they want you."

"WHAT? They want me to take a sorceress as a consort?"

"Ummm … yeah."

"A sorceress? The dreaded enemies of the Brotherhood for a thousand winters?"

"I know it's a lot to ask. The kingdom is at stake. If the demons attack our southern flank, we'll need the support of the Sorceri to survive."

"Have you discussed this alliance with the Counsel?"

"It was their idea."

"That's what Mar meant by my assignment."

"What do you mean?"

"Nothing. It's not important. What do you know of this woman they want me to bond with?"

"Not too much. She's the fifth daughter of the High Mage, a level five. Look at the bright side, your offspring would be quite magical."

"Great! Just what I wanted."

Timikia grew silent. It was clear he was weighing his options.

"When is this supposed to happen?" Timikia inquired.

"Soon. High Mage Fardarius is ready to move immediately. You'll need to start courting her daughter as soon as possible. Sorceri tradition dictates a half-winter courtship. She'll need this to get the

High Coven to vote for the alliance."

"It will take two or three moons for them to travel here," Timikia said. "That gives me time to warm up to the idea."

"Actually, they'll be using the portal. She could arrive in a sun or two."

"THE PORTAL! You opened up the portal to the Sorceri? They could use it to launch a surprise attack."

"They need this alliance as much as we do. We have to trust each other, at least for the time being. But trust only extends so far. I have tripled the guard around the portal."

"Well," Timikia said, sighing with resignation, "isn't this a nice welcome home present. Set it up."

"I do have a gift I think you'll like."

I retrieved the old, rusty key from my pocket and presented it to him.

"What's it open?"

"Follow me," I said with a smile.

We proceeded to the lower levels of the palace. As we descended, the dust and cobwebs grew thicker.

"I will have the staff come down here and clean this mess up," I said. "No one has been down here for quite some time."

Traversing down a narrow hallway, we reached a dark, unassuming door.

"Your key opens this door."

"What's behind it?"

"Lord Whispa's laboratory."

"Are you kidding me? Doesn't the Brotherhood confiscate all a lord's possessions upon his death?"

"They wanted to. Trust me—they wanted to. I told them I had never seen his lab. Which was partially true. As a woman, it's too dangerous for me to enter so I've never been in there. I've never … seen it."

"Over seven hundred winters of collecting, experimenting, probing the depths of the dark magic and it's mine?"

"I'm sure Lord Whispa would have wanted you to have it."

"I'm sure he does. I'll have to chat with him about it."

"What?"

"I've been speaking with him on the other side."

"WHAT? By the powers—honestly? Our Lord Whispa?"

"He's the only Lord Whispa I know. Heck, I'm not sure Atlantis could have handled two of him."

"If you've seen him, what about your father?"

"Not yet. Maybe some sun."

My heart sunk a bit. *What I would give to say "I love you, Timicus," one more time.*

Timikia inserted the key into the lock. It took two hands to turn through the grime and rust. The latch clunked open and the door creaked.

"I have a feeling you're going to be here a while," I said. "I'll ask one of the cooks to bring your dinner down here. Enjoy."

Chapter #17

The Gift

T he door was frozen, rusted shut. It took four kicks to swing it open. The windowless chamber was draped in darkness. The hallway light refracted through hundreds of glass vials and bathed the walls in an array of shadowy colors.

A large cabinet loomed to my right about twice my height and wider still. Its wooden handles were worn down to nubs as if opened thousands of times. As I tugged at the door, bottles rattled within. Holding up the lamp for a better look, I couldn't believe my eyes. Hundreds of healing potions in bottles of all shapes and sizes lined the shelves, a small fortune's worth.

A similar enclosure was erected to my left. Inside were enough flasks of poison to kill everyone in a midsize city. To my surprise, some of the potions weren't green. I had overheard rumors that Lord Whispa experimented with nontraditional toxins. This would deserve further investigation. But for now, other treasures awaited me.

Chemicals, dried herbs, and liquids lined the shelves of several workbenches. Beyond them was a large fire pit. There were no logs in the pit, only a crystalline, yellowish powder with a faint smell of sulfur. Curious, I ignited it. A tall flame shot up from the pit and illuminated the room with bright red and blue waves. I found it strange that the flames weren't hot. They were cold. Waving my hand through the blaze gave me a chill.

Now well lit, the room was larger than it first appeared. There was so much to see and explore. A large trunk was tucked into the corner. It didn't look like much, but simple containers often hold the greatest treasures. I struggled to lift the massive lid. And there it was—Lord Whispa's armor. The contents of this single chest were worth millions. Every piece so steeped in mythology and lore it had its own name. The real prize was the helmet, the Crown of Perendice. It bore the horns of a powerful creature and was so black it fought off the fire's light. Fearing to touch it, I remembered the stories of it being alive. Gathering my courage, I gently lifted it. The helm did not react to my touch. As I placed it on my head, the helm shrunk to a perfect fit.

"Ohhh, I look good in this," I said checking myself out in the mirror.

A small dagger lay on the workbench nearby. After picking it up, I considered my next action.

"Dare I? What the hell. Why not?"

I tried to jab the helmet with the dagger. The horns came to life, batting the weapon away. It left a large welt on the back of my hand.

"Awesome!"

There were other valuable items to discover within the chest: the spell resistant chest plate known as Defenden, gauntlets of unknown abilities, plated boots that extended over the knees, six daggers still glowing green with absorbed poison, a shrunken head shield, and both of Lord Whispa's wands—Wrecker and Witherer. I had seen those wands many times before. Each one was unique in the damage it inflicted. Wrecker preferred to shatter things, while Witherer aged them. Combined with my father's wand, I was creating quite an arsenal. There was also a wand holster. It was nothing special, just a simple leather sheath. I strapped it to my leg and placed my wand within. Realizing that I couldn't keep calling it my "father's wand," I needed to find a new name.

"Pain Monkey," I tried out. "No. No, that's stupid. What about— Soul Ripper? That doesn't even make sense. Banisher! Ooooh … I liked the sound of that. Well, wand, what do you think?"

In my mind, I saw the monkey head smile.

At the far end of the laboratory was a massive oak door. A hefty iron latch sealed it shut, but to my surprise there was no lock securing it. Placing my ear to the door, all was calm. It took both hands to flip the heavy latch. The door opened with a horrible grinding noise that rattled my teeth. In the darkness, a pair of red, glowing eyes peered out. I hastened to close the door. The skeleton roared as it pushed through. In a panic I emoted, blowing it back into the room. Three more skeletons emerged from the darkness. Armed with axes, the skels' made it clear I was their target.

I hoped to exploit their poor vision by retreating to the far side of the fire pit. The flames hid me from their view. I began backing out of the lab. Despite every attempt to be silent, I bumped into the cabinet causing the bottles of poison to clatter. The skels hissed in hate as they reacquired me. They walked straight through the frigid flames leaving icicles hanging from their bones.

Grabbing a vial, I chucked it in the face of the closest one. It writhed in agony as the green fluid splattered across its boney frame. It fell to the floor, convulsing. Using the curse of Dionissis, I blinded the other two. I only had moments before they would regain their senses. From thin air, I created a demon bone spear. Its golden glow hovered beside me. With a wave of my hand, I flung the spear shattering a skel's ribcage.

An ax cut deep into my thigh, slamming me to the ground. I encased the monster in a demon bone cage that grew up out of the ground and enveloped it. My blood gushed everywhere. Crawling to the other cabinet, I grabbed a healing potion. Ripping out the cork with my teeth, I guzzled it down. As my blood flow slowed, the bone prison dissolved around my captive, freeing the skeleton. Grabbing Banisher, I blew out its knee with a single cut. The skel crashed on top of me, waving its ax in a desperate attempt to strike. I jammed my wand into its mouth. The skull shook violently and crumbled.

Between my injury and the use of so many spells, I was drained. I lay on the floor panting. The first skeleton reappeared from its room brandishing a spear. I had just enough mana for one final spell. It had to be a good one. There on the floor lay the dagger that the helmet had torn from my hand. I focused my remaining energy in a swirl around it. The small weapon morphed up into a massive, bulky, iron golem green with the dagger's poison. I was always amazed at how little metal it took to create such a giant. Its huge shoulders glistened in the firelight. Thanks to Lord Whispa aligning me with a great warrior from the other side, I was able to imbue the metal monster with his soul.

"KILL IT!" I screamed.

My golem charged. The skel jammed its spear into him. The reflective power of the golem shot the spear's force back into the skeleton, blowing off its arm. The golem crushed its skull with one strike of his massive fist. His steely eyes turned to me. He rushed to my side, surveying my injury. Then, he reached for a healing potion.

"STOP!" I shouted. "Your big-ass fingers are going to smash the bottles. I'm good, I'm good. I got this now. Thank you. Thank you so much. So, what do you think? Our first battle together. Not too shabby, heh?"

I imagined he was smiling, even though his steel face could not.

"Are you ready to go back?"

Victus nodded. With my energy returning, I swirled the magic around him. His soul returned to the other side as the metal shell melted into a steely puddle.

"Well, that's a shame," I said to myself. "That was probably a pretty good dagger."

After drinking another potion, I felt well enough to stand on my injured leg.

"Thanks a lot, Lord Whispa," I spoke into the room as if he could hear me, "You could have at least warned me you had a minion pit down here."

As I surveyed the shattered bones at my feet, I wondered what these poor souls did to Lord Whispa to warrant such treatment. I knew angry necromancers would sometimes torment the souls of their minions. If they hated them in life, they could torture them in death. Lords occasionally bury their skels leaving the worms to feast on their bones.

Well, I thought, *that's more than enough for one sun.*

Turning to the door, I was startled by one of the palace cooks holding a dinner tray. I had no idea how long he had been standing there, but his face was white. He was shaking like a leaf in the wind.

"Are you okay?" I asked.

"It was … ah … live … alive … and then … it … ah … pop … ah … blood …"

Limping over to him, I put my arm around his shoulder. I comforted him with my smile.

"Let's go back to the kitchen," I said. "Just breathe. You'll be all right. It'll be all right."

Chapter #18

Her

"Look at you, all handsome in your shiny new armor."

"Mother," I said, "my hair is fine, you can stop trying to fix it."

"You want to look nice. It's not every sun you meet your future consort."

"Ah, yeah. I think I was better off meeting the skels in Lord Whispa's minion pit."

"Now, Timikia, I want you to have an open mind about this. She might be a lovely, young woman—"

"Or a horrible shrew. If she looks anything like the High Mage, yikes!"

"TIMIKIA, be nice. That is no way to talk about a High Coven member and your future mother-in-law. I thought I raised you better."

"But she's a sorceress. I've had nightmares about them."

"No buts. Give her a chance. She might surprise you."

I was not convinced. Mother and I took the trolley to the portal center to await my future consort's arrival. It was one of the kingdom's major sources of income. Normally, the center was bustling with travelers. On this sun, portal jumps had been suspended mainly out of security concerns. An assassination attempt would be disastrous.

Hundreds of the mostly elite had come to witness the historic event. Few lords could remember back to a sun when a portal between our clans was unlocked. They had spruced up the center for the occasion. The fresh paint, exotic flowers, and imported silk draperies brought an air of refinement to this normally drab location.

"Prince Timikia," asked the center's chief cleric, "would you do the honors of initiating the portal?"

"Yeah, why not."

I stepped up to the platform and scooped up a handful of the dust. Tossing it into the holy, red flame, it exploded in a blue glow. I spoke the source enchantment adding the name of our portal to the end of my phrasing. The blue dome opened up around the flame. With dark clouds looming, it was a welcome source of light. I articulated the target enchantment enriching it with the name of the Sorceri's portal. The dome pulsed thrice and the connection was completed. With a heavy heart, I had unlocked my kingdom to an ancient enemy. I returned to my seat, awaiting their arrival. Banisher was close at hand, just in case.

A page garbed in opulent robes emerged from the portal and stood proud at the top of the steps.

"All hail," he began, "the arrival of High Mage Fardarius."

I was about to clap when he continued.

"High council to the High Coven. Keeper of the Grand Key of Marowbius. Lead Sorceress to the Lakes of Persona ..."

This went on for a while. *How many titles can one person have*, I thought. *They had to be making these up.* When at last there was a break in the monologue, I raised my hands to applaud. And then he continued ...

"First daughter of High Mage Merinda. Hero of the battle of Kon. First seer of Mount Ariaus ..."

He traversed his way through fifteen generations. I was just about to nod off when High Mage Fardarius stepped out. Mother kicked my leg. Startled, I started clapping. Fardarius smirked at my inattentiveness.

"Now good people of Surdon," the page rambled on, "I am proud to introduce, Minor Mage Solendra. Class five sorceress. Class of Mariota master. Supervisor of ..."

Here we go again. What a bunch of blowhards. Somewhere in there, I'm sure they gave her shoe size.

"Minor Mage Solendra is the fifth daughter of High Mage Fardarius. High council to the High Coven. Keeper of the Grand Key of Marowbius. Lead Sorceress to the Lakes of Persona ..."

They had to be kidding. He was starting the whole generations thing over again? He repeated fifteen more generations of mind-numbing, useless crap. At long last, this insufferable pain came to an end.

Minor Mage Solendra stepped out of the haze. The blue glow of the portal bathed her in a halo that twinkled in my eye. Long, pin-straight, black hair framed her face like a painting. Her eyes were so dark they were almost void of light. Solendra's black bodysuit fit her tall, lean body like an extra skin. Her golden-brown skin was smooth and perfect, with soft pink lips that highlighted her face like an icing flower on a cake. Palace City suddenly seemed a bit brighter with her in it.

Whoa, I thought, *this might not be so bad after all.*

I climbed the steps to greet her. She did not present her hand, so I reached out and took it.

"Good sun, Mage Solendra," I said before kissing her hand. "I am Guardian Necromancer Timikia, Prince of Surdon. It is most pleasant to make your acquaintance."

She responded with a simple nod. Those eyes were enchanting. I led her to the trolley, which transported the two of us and our mothers back to the palace. There was no conversation the entire way. As awkward as that was, I barely noticed. I couldn't take my eyes off her, although I did my best not to stare.

A grand feast had been prepared—five courses of the best delicacies our renowned master chefs could concoct. The first course was Merandin goose livers sauteed in a cherry brandy. This was followed by jasmine infused spring pine hearts. My mouth salivated at the sight of our main course, braised wild boar. I ate too much and only picked at the assortment of slowly melted cheeses. The dessert did not disappoint as Verisian strawberries, imported by portal from the Vin Mountains, were dressed in sweetened goat cream and powdered with hazelnut dust. In spite of being full, I ate every last berry.

Solendra sat to the left of her mother. She seemed unimpressed by the meal. I sat three seats away to the right of the Queen, and I glanced over hoping to catch her eye. She stared straight ahead into the crowd, never returning my gaze.

Several kings of other kingdoms were in attendance as were several prominent lords, including Mar and Loter. Even though my mother had banned Loter from our kingdom, there was little she could do to prevent his entry when he showed up with ten other top lords, including five council members.

When dinner ended, my betrothed and I, along with our mothers, retired to a private room. The two rulers enjoyed light conversation, and there was no mention of politics or the treaty. After a short time, my mother patted my hand.

"High Mage Fardarius," Mother began, "let's leave these two

alone to get better acquainted."

"Excellent idea, my good Queen Lika. Perhaps you and I can find a quiet place to discuss military strategy."

"My council chambers would be a perfect setting. I will have the kitchen bring us some tea. Shall we go?"

The two monarchs departed leaving me sitting across the table from Solendra. I hadn't been this nervous since my pledge test when I was twelve.

"So, Solendra, wasn't that a lovely—"

"LISTEN NECRO!" Solendra spat, her eyes burning with hate. "I'm a loyal Sorceri and a grateful servant of the High Coven. I will play this stupid little game of theirs. I will go to your parties and attend your events. In public, I will be the perfect consort. But if you think for one breath you will EVER lay a finger on this body, you've got another thing coming. A level five is more than a match for some newly promoted guardian. I will keep my wand under my pillow at all times. If you so much as crack the door to my room, I will FRY YOUR ASS! The thought of having a mongrel child with a filthy, dark-magic-using demented monster like you makes my SKIN CRAWL! You've been warned to keep your distance and, while you're at it, keep your thoughts and mindless moronic opinions to yourself."

She shot to her feet flinging her chair back against the wall. With a sneer, she bolted from the room. My arms were tingling to the point I could barely feel my fingers. I sat stunned contemplating the disaster that had just unfolded before me. At long last, I decided to retire to my bed chambers, although I knew I wouldn't sleep.

Traversing the hallways to the east wing, I turned the corner straight into my next catastrophe.

"What do you want, Loter?"

"Still not calling me lord?"

"I'll call you that when you deserve my respect."

"You don't learn your lessons easily, do you, boy?"

"I'm in no mood for you tonight. What do you want?"

"Only one thing from you—the spell."

"What spell?"

"Let's not play games, boy. You know what spell I'm talking about. You're too smart to play dumb. I want that purple wall. It belongs to the Brotherhood. Surrender your book."

"No."

"Even with the wall spell, you are no match for me, kid. I don't have to ask. I could simply take it."

"Seriously," I chuckled, "you would attack the crowned prince in his own palace. You wouldn't make it back to the portal. So, I agree, let's stop playing games. Even if you could take the book, the spell isn't in it."

"You're telling me YOU created that spell?" Loter laughed. "A spell like that would take ten winters of research. You're not old enough or talented enough to accomplish that."

"True, my father did the bulk of the research, but he never got it to work. The book would be useless to you without my key calculations."

"You? A mere, lowly guardian figured it out?"

"Yeah—what do you think about that?"

"Do you realize a spell like that could shift the balance of power in the Brotherhood's favor?"

"I do. So did my father. I don't want to turn the Brotherhood into a conquering horde. We have enough of those in Atlantis. The spell stays with me."

"You're as foolish as your father was. Turning over that spell would buy you a lot of goodwill within the Brotherhood. Plus, you wouldn't want to risk being excommunicated, would you?"

"At this point, I could complete my training on my own. Even if the Brotherhood didn't grant me a lordship, I would still end up just as powerful. Plus, I doubt the Brotherhood would risk their precious alliance. The Sorceri wouldn't take kindly to the consort of their cherished daughter being excommunicated. You have overplayed your hand, Loter, and you know it."

Breaking eye contact, he grew quiet.

"You're going to need the Brotherhood, kid," Loter said. "No necromancer can survive alone. And some sun—you're going to need me too. Be careful what bridges you burn."

"I believe you have overstayed your welcome. I suggest you leave."

Loter withdrew in silence. I had stared into the jaws of the tiger and had not flinched. But who was my greatest concern—Loter or her?

Chapter #19

Courtship

"How did it go last night?" Mother asked.

I joined her at the breakfast table.

"Ohhhh … pretty bad. She shared her true feelings for me. In her eyes, I rank someplace between pond scum and a demon-dog. And closer to the demon-dog end of the spectrum."

Mother shared those empathic eyes of hers. They always made things a little better.

"Give her time," Mother explained. "This pairing was sprung on her as well. It will take a while for both of you to adjust. If I recall, you said a few disparaging remarks about her too before you even met her."

"That's a good point."

"Of course, it is. I saw her heading for the stables early this morning. The Sorceri do love their horses. I know it's been a while since you rode. Maybe you'd like to take a ride this morning. Finding something you both have in common would be a good start."

"You are so wise. No wonder the Brotherhood crowned you Queen. That's a good idea. I'll give it a try."

I didn't rush through breakfast though. I was secretly hoping Solendra wouldn't be there when I arrived. But she was. I found her riding circles around the training track. She clearly knew what she was doing. She rode with a confidence well beyond her winters. With each lap, she glanced at me for a moment before refocusing her attention on the horse. I motioned to the stable boy to bring out my favorite ride. When he arrived with Blackness, I walked him out onto the track. Solendra pulled up as she approached. I made the strategic decision to ignore last night's outburst. No good would come of dwelling on it.

"What do you think of your horse?" I asked.

"It's fair—I guess," she said.

"If I'm not mistaken, that's a Druid horse. They breed the finest animals in all of Atlantis."

"True enough," Solendra said. "I guess the problem must be with its training. A waste of a good animal."

If I could hold a wand for five hundred breaths in the room, surely, I could put up with this.

"Your horse is not Duridian," Solendra said. "What is it?"

"You have a good eye for horses. It's Barbarian. They are bigger and stronger. Better for combat."

"And it probably moves like a cow. Is that all you necros think about? Combat? I know that's all your magic is good for. Perhaps, I can import a couple of decent horses from home."

As a necromancer, I'm supposed to be good at controlling my emotions, but she was trying my patience. She rode off for another roundabout.

After mounting Darkness, I rode after her. If our horses strode side-by-side, she would see I too was a good horseman. Every time I almost caught her, she picked up her pace. Lap after lap, I tried to catch up, but damn she was right. Darkness couldn't keep up with the leaner animal in the turns. He did move like a cow. After ten laps of this futility, I stopped at the gate and dismounted. She trotted up.

"See, I told you. Even on this mediocre animal, I can outride the likes of you. You're just going to have to face it, Sorceri are better in every way."

She galloped off the track and into the fields.

I stroked Darkness's head. "You're still my favorite horse," I whispered in his ear.

Handing the reins to the stable boy, I marched back to the palace.

"That was quick," Mother said. "I assume it didn't go well."

"That girl is going to drive me insane. No one could tolerate her. She is so arrogant—so competitive."

Mother started laughing out loud.

"What's so funny?" I said with a moan. "I don't see anything funny about this situation."

"You hate in her what you see in yourself."

"What? I'm nothing like her."

"Oh nooo, you're not competitive at all—mister guardian at sixteen."

What is it with all these women in my life being right all the time?

"All right, I might be a little competitive," I replied.

"Really? Just a little?"

With a look only a mother can give, she saw right through me.

"I think you might have discovered what you have in common," she said.

"What? Being competitive?"

"Exactly. You can throw in bull-headed while you're at it."

"Hey!"

"You have to look at it from her point of view. When you first arrived at Nocmara, how did you feel?"

"Lost … confused."

"She probably feels the same way."

"It's hardly the same. Her posh sleeping quarters and three gourmet meals a sun is hardly a comparison to what I have had to endure."

"Still, she was ripped away from her life, her friends, her teachers and dragged off to live with a former enemy. I'm sure she feels as isolated as you did and probably just as afraid."

"I never thought about it like that."

"What if you challenged her? Gave her a goal—a reason to wake up in the morning. Striving to compete might allow her to see you in a new light. And perhaps … just maybe, you'll see her differently too."

"It's not going to be riding, I'll tell you that. She's way better than me."

"What is a necromancer superior at?"

"Combat. Killing stuff."

"All right, start there."

"You want me to kill her? Actually, not such a bad idea."

"No! But there has to be something you mastered at Nocmara, that she hasn't."

"Hmmm … I think I know just the thing."

***

As the morning light spread across the training track, Solendra arrived to find me standing in the middle of the circle. I thought I would take it slow with position one, my left foot perched on my right knee. I focused on my breathing and ignored her. She mounted her horse and warmed up by circling the track. After her third lap, she rode up to me. I did not make eye contact.

"WHAT are you doing?"

"Training."

"For what? Looking like an idiot? Trust me, you're already a master at that."

"It's combat training."

"How is perching on one leg combat? How the Sorceri didn't conquer you necros centuries ago is a mystery."

She rode off for more laps. I did not break position or focus. I behaved as if she wasn't there. After a short time, she approached again. Still, I made no eye contact.

"How is that combat training?" she asked again.

"Balance makes for a better warrior."

With a snicker, she drew her wand. "This makes a better warrior. Spells make you a better warrior."

"Perhaps."

"Watch and learn, necro."

Her eyes glowed as she crossed her arms in front of her face. With a violent motion, a blast of blue light shot from her wand and enveloped a nearby target, coating it in a layer of ice.

"Impressive," I said, "but can you hit the target at a full gallop?"

"Of course, I can."

"If you say so."

She rode off in a huff. As she passed the target, she fired again and missed. Another pass, another miss. On the third try, she found the target.

"See, I told you," Solendra said.

"Pretty good, but can you hit the target from the far side of the ring?"

Doubt flickered in her eyes as she glanced at the far rail.

"No one could make that shot!"

"I could."

"Prove it!"

"Normally, I would never use magic for show, but I'll make an exception in this case."

I motioned for the stableboy to fetch Blackness. After mounting the massive steed, I guided him to the far rail, and then I rode the width of the track three times before launching the bone spear. It struck true, shattering her ice and splintering the wood. With a smile, I dismounted and returned to the palace with no more than a glance in her direction. I wasn't exactly gloating, but I wasn't exactly not.

Early the next sun, I arrived to find Solendra in the center of the ring. She quivered to and fro in a desperate attempt to hold position one. After walking out to her, I assumed position one with ease. Her frustration permeated the air. As the sun rose into the sky, she began improving.

"See," she said, "anything a necro can do a sorceress can do. This isn't so hard."

"Very good. Try closing your eyes."

"What?"

"Try it with your eyes closed."

Within a moment, she lost her balance and found herself butt down on the ground.

"ARGH!" she screamed pounding her fists into the sand. "JUST … JUST …. ARGH!" She stormed out of the stables.

I don't pride myself on gloating, I thought, *but, it's sort of fun.*

Later that night, I walked past her chambers to discover her practicing. For two more suns, I watched her struggle, but her determination was impressive. On the third sun, she had mastered it with her eyes closed.

"See, I can do it," she said with a smirk.

"Nice. Try this one."

I stretched out into position three. Her eyes narrowed and her jaw tightened. In a fit of rage, she shoved me to the ground.

"YOU'RE DOING THIS ON PURPOSE!"

"Doing what?"

"You're trying to make a fool out of me."

"I'm confused. I thought Sorceri could do anything a necro could do?"

"YEAH! WELL—I still ride better than you."

"That you do. What do you say we strike a deal?"

"What kind of deal?"

"You teach me to ride. I'll teach you how to stand here and look like an idiot—without falling on your ass."

Conflicting emotions flashed across her face.

"Fine. I'll agree to that."

"Fantastic. At this point, your legs are probably quite tired. What do you say we start on horseback?"

Over the next moon, we rode and balanced every morning. The conversation began turning from stilted instructions to more civil topics. One sun, we actually had lunch together. That wasn't as miserable as I thought it would be. One cool morning, while returning from a particularly hard ride, our relationship took a turn.

"You're getting better, Timikia. You traversed that last set of tight turns like a champ. Even if you do ride a cow."

"I have a good instructor."

"That you do," she said. "Race you back to the stables?"

I didn't answer, I just put Darkness into a full sprint. If I was going to have any chance against her, I needed an advantage. She caught up as we entered the path through the forest. We were riding neck and neck as we approached the fork in the path. She used her superior skills to steer me to the left. I knew what she was up to. She was edging me toward the river jump. Darkness always refused to hurdle it.

"Come on, Darkness. You can do it!"

Much to my surprise, Darkness attempted the jump, bounding over the water. His massive frame pressed his hooves deep into the mud. Solendra bolted ahead to the training track. Turning she watched me come in second—as usual.

"Not bad! Not bad at all for a necromancer," Solendra laughed.

"Thank you."

"What? For saying you're not bad?"

"No … for referring to me as a necromancer and not a necro."

She grew quiet.

Chapter #20

Understanding

I was ashamed. Not since failing my level three wand test, have I felt this bad. Prince Timikia was right. Everyone in the palace has been nice to me and I had been nothing but rude. I thought I was disgracing everyone else. In truth, I was disgracing myself. What kind of ambassador of the Sorceri was I?

As I walked to the kitchen, I passed the Queen's chambers. She and Timikia were eating dinner at her desk, an odd place to dine. I wanted to join them, but I was fearful of the Queen's reaction. After all, I insisted on eating every meal alone since my mother returned home after the celebration dinner. I don't deserve to break bread with her now. The Queen must hate me. If Timikia told her half the nasty things I've said to him, she would be well within her rights to despise me.

I couldn't make out what they were saying, but their tone was somber. Sneaking closer to the door, I listened in. Were they discussing the alliance? The demons? Something more serious? I wanted to know. Being nothing more than a figurehead did not land well with me. If this palace was ever to be my home, I needed to know what was going on, even if I had to spy.

"Are you sure you want to start tonight?" Queen Lika asked.

"The sooner I start, the sooner I finish," Timikia replied.

"It's not uncommon for guardians to take as much as two winters off," Queen Lika said.

"The kingdom—my kingdom—is facing many threats. I need to complete the journey."

"I wish I knew what you were about to face. I have never witnessed it." There was a quiver in the Queen's voice.

"Few outside the Brotherhood have."

"Are you sure you can't return to Nocmara, at least for the first few moons?"

"I don't trust Loter or Mar for that matter. I'm better off here—alone."

"It sounds so risky. Are you sure?"

"Don't worry. I have all of Lord Whispa's notes and his guidance. I'll be fine."

He stood and kissed her forehead. I ducked behind a pillar as he exited the chambers. The Queen was openly weeping.

What is going on? I thought. *This sounds bad.*

In the hidden shadows, I followed Timikia through the halls. The palace staff found my actions disturbing but failed to alert Timikia to my presence. He traveled to a part of the palace I had never seen, to an old staircase.

The boots of my battle suit were padded with a magical substance. With those, I can prance in almost total silence. That would have been helpful had I been wearing them. Unfortunately, one does not don battle garb to go to dinner. My court shoes had hard leather soles that made a slight tap with each step. I had to wait until Timikia cleared a flight before I could follow. At the bottom of the steps was a long hallway. As I hid at the exit of the stairwell, all I could do was listen. The sound of tumblers in an iron lock fell as a door opened. Hinges creaked and his footsteps were muffled as the door closed behind him.

I glided down the hallway. Timikia had left the key in the lock, the sign of a man distracted. The thickness of the door made it difficult to hear. The clinking of glass broke the silence. Timikia let out a great sigh, followed by more silence. Then—the gagging—so much gagging, followed by the sound of Timikia puking. Next, came the thud of a body hitting the stone floor.

I threw the door open. Timikia was on all fours hovering over a pool of vomit. Green veins pulsed across his face. I stepped in to help.

"STOP!" Timikia screamed. "NO CLOSER!"

"I can help you!"

He gagged again, spitting up blood.

"GET OUT!"

Timikia emoted and blew me back into the hall. Blasting again he slammed the door shut with his magic.

For a few moments, I was frozen in panic. I dashed up the stairs to the kitchen.

"Help! Help! Somebody, help!"

My outburst stunned the staff.

"Prince Timikia is ill in the cellar. Get a healer. Call for a lord. Get help!"

They looked at one another and returned to their kitchen duties.

"ISN'T ANYONE GOING TO DO SOMETHING!"

They all ignored me. I dashed off to the Queen's chambers. I found her sitting at her desk.

"My Queen, Timikia is gravely ill. Come quick."

I started for the door when she grabbed my arm.

"Solendra, please, have a seat."

"You don't understand. Timikia might be dying."

"He might be dead, but there is nothing we can do. Please sit. Let me explain."

Queen Lika returned to her chair, her eyes still red from tears. She motioned to the chair in front of the desk. I was confused but did as she requested.

"Timikia has begun the poisoning," Queen Lika said.

"The WHAT?"

"The poisoning. Now that you live with us, you need to know the whole truth about necromancers. It takes a guardian as long as sixty winters to become a lord."

"That's impossible. No one lives that long."

"Exactly. For guardians to live long enough to complete their training, they have to extend their lives. That's why they commit to the poisoning. Every few suns, they ingest a small amount of poison. As you've already seen, it makes them quite sick. One in five guardians dies in the process. Another two fifths can't take it and quit. Eventually, they become immune. Later still, their bodies begin creating the poison from within. At that point, they become living venomous weapons. They can expel it from their skin. The poison greatly extends their lives. The process can take decades to complete. It is quite common for a lord to live seven hundred winters or more once they have completed the poisoning. Timikia's mentor lived to eight hundred and nineteen before he passed to the other side."

"Timikia poisoned himself?" I inquired.

"Yes. The first few moons are the worst."

"So … he might die tonight?"

"Yes. Or the next time. Or the time after that. Every poisoning is a risk."

"I want to go down and help him."

"You can't. We should have warned you about Timikia's laboratory when you arrived. You must never enter that room."

"I'm not a spy. I'm not trying to steal the magic."

"It has nothing to do with trust. It's the poison itself. Necromancer poison is toxic to all creatures, but females are highly susceptible. Even the dried dust on the floor could kill you within moments."

"Why is it so much more dangerous for women?"

"The Brotherhood doesn't know for sure. It's assumed that the childbearing parts of our bodies are the cause."

"So that's why there are no women necromancers? The Coven told us it was because men are power-hungry animals and won't share with women."

"In the beginning, a number of women were admitted to the training. To their credit, many were promoted to guardian. Every last one of them died within a few suns of the poisoning. After that, the Brotherhood banned the training of women."

"That explains something else too."

"What is that, my dear?"

"Back home there is a museum of old weapons and armor. All the armor from the suns of the Necro Wars is poison resistant. I always wondered why. Now, I know."

"That is the way of war. One side makes a weapon, the other side creates a defense and the cycle continues. No one wins but the craftsmen making the weapons."

"When will we know if he survived?"

"If he is at breakfast, we will see his bright smile again. If he's not—"

"I don't understand. If it's so dangerous, why do it? Guardians are good warriors. What's wrong with just being a guardian?"

"Guardians are good fighters, but compared to a lord, they are nothing. One lord is worth twenty guardians. Lord Whispa fought in the Necro Wars—or as we call it, the Sorceri Darkenings. He told me it was commonplace for as many as ten sorcerers to attack one lord. Sorcerers complete their training quickly, so there are many more of them. How long does it take?"

"You can become a level seven or eight in six winters," I said.

"A fledgling can spend ten winters or more just to be promoted to guardian. Timikia did it in four, but when it comes to the poisoning, all bets are off."

"I don't think I'm going to be able to sleep tonight."

"Me neither. We're both going to have to get used to this. If not, we are in for a lot of sleepless nights."

We sat up and kept each other company.

Chapter #21

The Morning After

A s always, the food looked excellent. Although, all I could do was poke it with my fork. The sun was completely over the horizon, and still, Timikia was a no show. The Queen sat on my right and Soronto, her first handmaiden, on the left. No one had spoken since we sat down. I don't know why I cared so much—he was just a necromancer after all. If he died, I could go home. Still, every breath felt like an eternity.

"Can't we go check on him?" I asked.

"No," the Queen replied.

"If it's just about the poison, can't we send one of the men to check on him?"

"No. The poisoning is a private event and a vulnerable one. Necromancers pride themselves on their strength. They loathe being seen in a weakened state. We just have to wait—and have faith."

"Did you have to endure this with your consort, Timikia's father?"

"No, he was well past the poisoning stage when we met. He was a hundred and seventeen winters old and a full-fledged lord by then."

The staff cleared the table and still no Timikia. I didn't want to go home. Much as I hated to admit it, I was beginning to like it here. The grounds were lovely. The palace library was quite extensive. It felt nice to ride for pleasure instead of the constant demands of training back home.

"TIMIKIA!" I shouted.

"Good morning," said the Prince.

I jumped up to hug him when I noticed the Queen and Soronto had not moved. I slowly sat back down. Why did I want to embrace him anyway? I didn't understand my feelings.

"It looks like I missed breakfast."

"Not a problem," said the Queen as she motioned to the staff.

He looked pretty good for a guy who nearly died the night before.

"What happened to you last—"

Queen Lika held up a hand to halt my inquiry. The look on her face said it all. We were not to speak of such things.

"Timikia," Queen Lika began, "what are your plans for this sun?"

"I think I'm going to skip my ride this morning. I don't feel up to it. Perhaps, I'll study more of Lord Whispa's book. I'm only about a quarter of the way through, and it's fascinating. He was a real potions master, which I never knew."

"Sounds like a good idea," Queen Lika said. "I'll have to excuse myself. I have duties to attend to. Soronto, I have need of you, so please join me. Solendra, why don't you keep Timikia company while he finishes breakfast. It is not pleasant to eat alone."

I knew what she was up to, and I'm guessing Timikia probably knew as well. She wanted to give us time to talk. I hoped some sun I would have half of her grace.

As the two women departed, I could see Timikia was deep in thought. He stared down at his plate while wringing his hands. I had no idea what the protocol was for this situation, so I stayed silent. I gave him time to gather his thoughts.

"I'm sorry," Timikia said.

"For what?"

"Using magic on you."

"I understand why you did. You were trying to save my life."

"Still—"

"Don't give it another thought. I'm sorry, too."

"For spying on me?"

"Yes, I overheard you and your mother talking and I was worried."

"Worried about ME?"

"Yeah. I know it's crazy, right?"

"Maybe not. When I saw you at the door, despite everything I was going through, all I could think of was keeping you out. You see, the floor was covered in—"

"I already know. Your mother explained it to me last night. It was an informative talk. I finally understand why there are no women necromancers."

"Yeah, we have reasons for what we do. It's not like the Sorceri."

"What do you mean 'It's not like the Sorceri'?"

"All sorcerers are women. That's the way the Coven wants it. So, that's the way it is."

"No! There have been male sorcerers."

"I've never heard of one."

"That's because they all go insane. They turn into homicidal maniacs. Good men kill their families, lay waste to entire villages, and worse. Now and then a man steals a wand. It doesn't take long before the Coven has to hunt him down like a rabid dog."

"Why is that?"

"No one knows. Some say it's because men are mentally unstable. Others, that they can't handle the power. That's why when I arrived, I was afraid of you."

"You feared me?"

"If the magic of the light could corrupt a man's mind like that, I figured dark magic must have turned you into a monster. I mean, your magic was stolen from the demons, right?"

"Yes, that's true."

"I don't know how you do it. How does that evil not corrupt your soul?"

Timikia picked up a bread knife and examined it.

"If I take this knife and cut some bread with it," he explained, "that's a good thing, would you agree?"

"Yes."

"If I slit your throat with it …"

Out of instinct, I felt for my wand.

"That's a bad thing, would you agree?" he continued.

"Yes."

"The knife is neither good nor bad. It's just a knife. It's what you do with it that determines whether it's evil or not. Necromancer magic is the same. It's just a tool. Care for a piece of bread?"

That made me laugh. I withdrew my hand from my holster.

"Since we've finally broached the subject of magic," I said, "how is it that you perform magic without a wand? You always carry it close, as do I, but you don't seem to need it."

"Our wands are just one of many tools of the trade. It's a good weapon, but no more than that. I have watched you perform magic. You're always using a highly polished, metal wand. I've assumed it's an energy focal point."

"That's exactly right. The wands are made of very expensive, rare Agrarian steel. It allows us to channel our mana down the shaft and collect it at the tip before launching. Only a few mages in the Coven are entrusted with the secret of how to make them."

"Necromancer wands are quite different. Our wands are alive."

"What? It's just a skull on a stick."

"I know, but sometimes late at night I can hear it whispering."

"That is really creepy."

"That it is. That it is. But it has never failed me."

"I was told stories about necromancers as a young girl. They were frightening tales of destruction and terror. Over the last few moons, I have not seen any of that behavior from you. I'm starting to believe I've been lied to."

"Truth is a strange phenomenon. Much of it depends on your perspective. The Necromancer-Sorceri Wars went on for a long time. When the carnage was over, all communication between our clans ceased. Over the centuries, the narrative got twisted to fit our individual biases. I, too, thought the worst of you before you arrived."

"Yeah," I said with a snicker, "and then I got here and proved you were right."

"Maybe at first," he smiled. "I saw you through my filter of hate. My mother had no such biases. She asked me to see you differently. You and I may never see eye-to-eye on much, but I think we have grown to respect each other. And isn't that the way peace is formed?"

Chapter #22

And So It Begins

"**Y**ou're late, my Prince."

As I stood in a perfect vibrationless position three, with my eyes closed no less. I could tell he was impressed. It was the first time I had worn my battle suit since I arrived. The tight embrace of the steel woven wool reminded me of home.

"And you're early," Timikia replied. "Your suit shimmers in the dawn's light. How does it do that?"

"It's made of a cloth known as sorijo. Only the Sorceri know how to weave it. It's almost as strong as plate armor but lighter and far more flexible. Watch."

With graceful motions, I slid into position four with ease.

"Very impressive."

"The battle suit or my balance?"

"All three, actually. The suit, your balance, and you. Over the last few moons, your balance has greatly improved. You've progressed much faster than I did."

His words made me smile.

"You know," I began, "you and I have never practiced crossing wands."

"OHHHH—now I get it. You come in here armored up and I'm in a tunic. Nice."

"Don't worry, I'll limit the power of my wand. It won't hurt—much."

"I can't do that. I don't control the power of my strikes. Banisher is in command of that. And I'm not sure he likes you."

"Excuses. Excuses. Come on, one touch."

Timikia stepped over to a maintenance bin and pulled out two wooden dowel rods.

"Let's use these instead," he said.

He tossed one to me. I had barely caught it when he lunged.

"So, that's how you're going to play it," I said. "Let's see how you deal with this."

It was my best move. I faked to the head, fainted to the chest, spinning and kneeling to cut to the back of his leg. When I finished my move, he was nowhere in sight. My mage senses alerted me to his presence behind me. Raising my stick over my head I blocked his strike. Rolling to avoid his next blow, I regained my footing.

"You're pretty nimble," I said with a smile, "for a man."

"And you're fast—you know—for a woman," he chuckled.

I cut to his head. He ducked. I swung for his legs. He leapt over the stick. Grabbing my arm, he spun me around setting up for a back strike. Taking advantage of his energy, I whirled through and pressed the stick to his neck. It was then I discovered his stick against my throat. Our faces were within a breath of each other. I never realized how blue his eyes were. His arm was tight around my waist as his eyes twinkled.

"It's good we're not using the real items," he said. "Care to go again?"

I pulled away, staring at the ground to avoid eye contact.

"Perhaps we should move on to riding."

"As you wish. What will you be schooling me on this sun?"

"Let's just ride for pleasure. That would be a nice change of pace."

As we rode out of the stables, toward the southern fields, I sprung the news on him.

"I have a surprise for you," I began.

"A surprise? A good one or a bad one?"

"Ahhh … depends on how you look it."

"So, it's probably a bad one."

"Well, my mother is visiting this sun."

"Your mother?"

"Yeah, and it gets worse. She's asked several Council Lords to be in attendance, including Lord Loter."

"Great. When was somebody going to tell me?"

"It was short notice. We only found out last night. I asked your mother if I could be the one to tell you."

"High Mage Fardarius wouldn't have invited Council members

without a good reason. What's so important?"

"Mother wants a report on how our courtship is going. I'll be the first one to speak to her about it."

"I see. What are you going to tell her?"

"The truth."

Timikia strode ahead to block my path, bringing us to a halt. Our eyes locked for several breaths.

"And what is the truth?"

"I have found you to be a good man."

"And ..."

"I can see myself living here."

He maneuvered his mount a few steps closer to me.

"And ..."

"And ... you're a strong leader who will be a good king some sun."

He moved side by side with me.

"And ..."

"And ... I ..."

He leaned towards me. My breath quickened. My heart raced. He gazed at me as if he was looking into my soul. I found myself leaning toward him as if drawn by magic.

"Help! Help me ..."

Timikia spun to confront the voice emanating from the trees. A beaten, bloodied soldier crawled out from the woods. Timikia leapt off this horse to aid him. The man was covered in wounds, some infected and spewing puss.

"Damn," Timikia said, "all my healing potions are back in my lab. Hang on, soldier, we're going to get you some help."

He coughed up blood and went limp.

"Stand back," I commanded, "I can help him."

As I drew my wand, I started my spell. Healing was not my best incantation. That's what held me back from level six.

"I'm losing him. I'M LOSING HIM! Damn, he's gone. I'm sorry. I tried."

"He was one of General Jaker's men," Timikia said. "Those troops were guarding the trench. He is far from the border. I need to know what he knows. Solendra, turn away. Better yet, take the horses over there by the trees. I don't want you to see this."

"I am not some prissy little princess you have to protect. I have been in battle. Do what you need to do."

"Have it your way. You were warned."

Looking down, he spoke to the corpse.

"You were a loyal soldier to the crown. You don't deserve this, but I have to know. I am sorry for what you're about to endure."

Timikia balled up his fists, and they glowed with a blue haze. His eyes sparked as the skin of the corpse jerked upward. The body's flesh began to melt and stream down exposing most of his bones. The skull hissed as its eyes dried up in their sockets and glowed a crimson red. The bones stood while the skin dripped off in a bubbling ooze.

"By the gods," I cried, "what is that thing?"

"I warned you to turn away."

"You created that thing?"

"Shhhh—I have to focus. I have to read him."

"Read him? What?"

"Please be silent. I need to concentrate."

A blue haze drifted from Timikia's eyes as the mana escaped. I had never seen such an intense look on any face in my life.

"Oh no," Timikia said. "They're here. They're here."

With a violent sweep of his arm, Timikia shattered the skeleton into a pile of bones at his feet.

"We have to go," said Timikia. "We have to ride."

"Wait! What? Talk to me."

Running and then mounting Darkness, he took off in a full sprint leaving me behind. I shot off after him. Normally, my steed was faster, but not this sun. Timikia drove Darkness with a blind fury, disregarding everything I had taught him. He tore past the stables and headed toward the palace. He rode straight past the guards and into the building itself like a madman. I dismounted outside and ran to join him.

"WHERE IS THE QUEEN? WHERE IS SHE?" Timikia screamed.

The startled guards pointed to the Queen's chambers. By this time, I was only a few steps behind. I had never seen him like this. My once calm, stable Timikia was acting like a crazed animal. He ran to the chambers and smashed through the doors. Inside stood the Queen, my mother, Lord Mar, Lord Loter, and a third, unknown to me, lord.

"HOW DARE YOU!" Mother exclaimed. Turning to the Queen, she hissed, "Is this how you've raised your son? He has the manners of a farm animal."

"THEY'RE HERE!" Timikia shouted.

"What? Huh—what?" Queen Lika said.

"The Blackhearts! They're upon us."

"Blackhearts?" questioned Lord Loter. "How do you know this, boy?"

"I raised and read a dead soldier. He was stationed with General Jaker and was assigned to patrol the trench. The Blackhearts dug their pit and surprised them from behind. What's left of the General's men are scattered in the hills. The wounded soldier rode three suns straight until his mount died. He's been crawling north ever since, trying to warn us."

"Blackhearts rarely fight alone," Lord Loter explained. "There could be a legion or two of cons, scourges or worse. What was the fate of the necromancer camp?"

"It's unclear. His commander sent him north with the message and he bolted from the battlefield. He needed to warn us that the demons have a powerful new general."

"Not another bug," Lord Loter said. "I thought we destroyed them all."

"No. This one walks on two legs, but it wields the black arts."

"We need to prepare quickly," Lord Mar said. "The demons could be within suns of the city walls. High Mage Fardarius, take the portal home and organize your forces."

"I'm sorry, but no."

"What do you mean no?" inquired Lord Loter.

"The Prince and my daughter have not been paired yet. No pairing. No alliance. I'm sorry, but the Brotherhood is on their own."

"Why you sneaky little ..." Lord Loter went for his wand.

Mother drew her wand and ignited it. Lord Mar planted his hand against Lord Loter's chest.

"Easy. Easy there," he said to Lord Loter. "So that's it? You're just leaving?"

"Yes." She took my hand. "Come, my daughter, we must depart immediately."

"NO!" I said, yanking my hand away. "Oh, aren't you the grand one? All my life, you've been lying to me. All your talk about how the Sorceri were better than EVERYONE ELSE, and the first chance you get you cut and run. It was all a steaming pile of lies."

"I have never lied to you."

"What about how all necromancers or necros as you call them, are nothing more than dark magic-soaked monsters? I've been so stupid. I've bought into the whole package, and I swallowed every word.

Now, I see the truth. The only monster in this room is you."

"Silence girl. We will discuss this back home. Now, do as I say."

"No! I'm done being your little puppet, dancing on a string every time you bark."

"By Coven law, until your pairing sun, you belong to me. You will OBEY!"

"Until I'm paired, huh?"

I took Timikia's hand and led him to Lord Loter.

"As a member of the Council you have the authority to pair a couple, am I right?"

"That is normally the task for clerics," he replied, "but technically, yes I can."

"Then, do it."

He addressed Timikia, "you've witnessed how untrustworthy sorcerers are. Are you sure you want to go through with this?"

Timikia gazed into my eyes and squeezed my hand tightly.

"Yes. Yes, I am," he said. "Some sorcerers can be trusted."

"Then kneel," Lord Loter commanded.

"Solendra, no! I forbid it," Mother commanded.

"In a moment you will no longer have the power to forbid me of anything. I will be free of you."

"Solendra, stop! The pairing will mean nothing. The truth is—the truth is—the Coven has no troops to send."

"What?" expressed Queen Lika.

"It's true. After winters of skirmishes with the Farcon, their hit and run tactics have scattered our forces all over Farondow. It would take us moons to even assemble a battalion."

"What about the High Coven?" I asked. "What about the Coven guards? Can't they come?"

"You can't expect Sorceri royalty to fight another clan's wars."

"I can and I do."

"Well, trust me—they're not going to come."

"So, just another lie in a long string of them. What was the plan? If the demons attacked the Coven, the Brotherhood would fight your war. If they attacked the Brotherhood, you'd find a way to weasel out of it?"

"Not exactly. The Coven would have honored the treaty if we had more time to prepare. No one thought the demons would attack this quickly. We can't afford to waste Sorceri in a lost cause."

"Lord Loter," I said, "please complete the pairing."

"There is no point, my child," he responded. "Even if the Coven honored their word and signed the alliance, no help is coming."

"There is a point, my Lord. I would like to stay and fight by my man. Better that than return to Farondow and hide in the shadows with cowards."

"Solendra, please," Mother begged. She tried to grab me, but Lord Mar blocked her path.

"My Lord," I said, "please continue."

"Timikia?" Lord Loter inquired.

He nodded as a small tear trickled down his cheek. He interlocked his fingers with mine and held on tightly.

And so, it came to pass that a daughter of the Coven and a son of the Brotherhood were bonded for life.

Chapter #23

Chain of
Command

"Face one another," Loter said. "May your souls always be entwined."

I was an emotional mess. Was she doing this out of duty, honor, or just to spite her mother? Why was I doing this? All I know is when I looked into her eyes, it felt right.

"Kiss her, you idiot," Loter barked.

Cupping my hands around the back of her neck, I pulled her close. Her lips were like silk. My heart fluttered.

"You betrayed your sisters," Fardarius said with venom. "You betrayed the Coven and most of all you betrayed me."

She tried to slap Solendra. I snagged her wrist like a mongoose snapping up a cobra's head.

"No one touches my consort while there's breath in me."

"How dare you! I could snuff you out like a candle," she boasted.

In defiance, Loter folded his arms. "Do you think you could snuff me out?"

Fardarius snorted as she yanked her hand away.

"You are no longer my daughter!"

"I can live with that," said Solendra.

The High Mage stormed out of the chambers.

"See, kid, I told you you'd need me some sun," Lord Loter said with a wry smile. "We have wasted enough time. Lord Mar, head back to Nocmara and rally the brothers. Bring every lord, every guardian, and the best of the fledglings."

"Fledglings?" said a shocked Lord Mar. "If we get wiped out here, that could be the end of the Brotherhood."

"Surdon is the gateway to the entire Southern Realm. If this kingdom falls, the Brotherhood is doomed anyway. We need to make our stand here and now."

With a nod, Lord Mar departed.

"Queen Lika, your people love you like no other ruler. I need you to rally them to your side."

"They are simple folk, not fighters," Mother replied.

"But they are hard workers. Do you have any engineering teams in the city?"

"Yes, we have four projects in construction now."

"Perfect. We need them to bolster the walls, reinforce the gates, and clear the grounds out to the edge of the forest. Your subjects can help. We need to turn that area into a killing zone. Time is of the essence."

"I understand. I will see to it personally." She gathered her skirts and strode out.

"Lord Kopla, take a handful of soldiers and scout the countryside. The more warning we can get about the demons' movements the better off we will be."

"I will be off within a tenth sun."

This left only Lord Loter, Solendra, and me.

"I want you to answer one question honestly," Lord Loter said to me. "Can you do that?"

"Yes."

"As the senior military leader of the Council, I will be in charge of all necromancers in this conflict. You and I have had our differences, but there must be a solid chain of command or all is lost. So, I ask you in all seriousness, are you loyal to the Brotherhood?"

"Yes."

"And will you follow my orders even to the end?"

"Yes."

"Good. Then this is what I require of you. With all your senior officers either lost or dead, your city guards will be looking to you for guidance. The necromancers will follow me without question, but your soldiers are loyal to you. You must inspire them. Convince them that we can win this battle. Get them to commit every drop of their sweat and blood to defend these walls. Do you think you can do that?"

"Yes, my Lord."

"That's good. That's very good, kid—I mean, Guardian Timikia."

"And you," Lord Loter said to Lady Solendra. "What can be done with a single level-five sorceress?"

"I will be the captain of Prince Timikia's personal guard."

"No," I responded.

"Oh yes, I will. Don't argue or we're going to have our first fight as a bonded pair."

"I need you for a more important task."

"More important than keeping you safe?"

"Much more. Most of our battle horses are at the trench or other borders. The stables are mostly full of pleasure rides, animals hardly fit for battle. I need you to work with the stable master to get as many of them ready for war as possible. You have a unique understanding of horses. I can't think of anyone better for the job."

"Great," Lord Loter said. "Now that we have that settled, I have a war to run. I'll leave you two lovebirds alone to say your goodbyes."

"I'll prepare the horses," said Solendra, "but when the fighting starts, I'm by your side."

"I love you too," I replied.

A tear welled up in her eye as she put her head on my shoulder.

"When you said you 'read' the soldier," Lady Solendra asked, "what did you mean by that?"

"When a necromancer reanimates a corpse, we create a thought connection between us. We can see through their eyes, hear with their ears, and know their last thoughts."

"So, he told you what happened in your head?"

"Not exactly. I don't hear them speak; I relive their memories. I was there on the battlefield, watching his friends being torn limb from limb by the blackhearts. That's an image I'll never be able to purge from my mind."

"My poor, Timikia. I never realized how hard it is to be a necromancer."

She squeezed me tight.

"What's a blackheart?" she asked.

"You don't know? At Nocmara, I had an entire class dedicated to learning every nuance of our enemies, both above and below ground. To defeat your enemy, you have to know them. Besides learning to fight, what did you learn back home?"

Lady Solendra drew her wand and started painting the air with bright strands of light. In a few breaths, she had drawn a beautiful flower that lit up the room like the sun. It hung in the air for a few moments, and then disbursed.

"I know," Lady Solendra said, "pretty useless, huh? A lot of good a glowing rose is going to be when you're fighting monsters."

"Blackhearts aren't monsters. They were once people, just like you and me. We created them."

"The Brotherhood made those things?"

"No. In a manner of speaking, both the Brotherhood and the Coven created them together. During the first Sorceri Darkening ... um ... Necromancer-Sorceri Wars ... a group of refugees hid in the underground labyrinth. The war went on so long they learned to live down there. The war—our war—drove them down there. Over thousands of winters, they changed. Their skin turned white, their hair black, and their eyes pale and lifeless. They became expert miners and earth workers. The most unique thing about them is they have two thumbs on each hand. It gives them incredible grip strength. Never let one get a hold of you because if they do, you will never get them off."

"I'd get them off. I'd just kill them," said Solendra.

"That would make it worse. Their hands are not built like ours. At rest, our hands open, theirs clench into a fist. In death, they squeeze even tighter. But they do have one major weakness, their eyes. They can see in almost total darkness, but in the light—that's a different story. Your glowing flower might save your life some sun."

"Or yours."

"Or mine. Now go and tend to those horses. I have soldiers to prepare."

After one more kiss, I watched her walk away. I didn't want to let her go. I bet this wasn't how she pictured her bonding sun.

"It's time," I whispered to myself.

I walked down the worn steps to my lab. I lit the blue flame and opened the trunk.

The boots were solid enough, but if Lord Whispa kept them in this trunk, they must be special. Too bad I never got around to asking him. The fingertips of the gauntlets came to sharp killing points, perfect for a hand-to-hand brawl. The breastplate seemed too light to stop an arrow or sword. It shimmered like Lady Solendra's bodysuit.

"Could it have been made by the Sorceri?" I wondered.

The thigh-plates had built-in sheaths, one for each of Lord Whispa's wands. I placed Banisher on the right. Unlike Lord Whispa, I could only hold one wand at a time, but having a spare at the ready could be useful. Both of Lord Whispa's wands were legendary, so which would be the best backup? Wrecker was powerful but similar to Banisher. Plus, I already had a relationship with Banisher. Wrecker's box was tucked in the upper-right corner of the trunk. It was a plain box with a mother-of-pearl letter "I" inlaid on the top, a simple box for such a powerful relic. Wrecker's crown was a baby fox skull and the stem was polished stone. It fought me as I picked it up. The pain was bearable, but might be a distraction in battle. *Not a good choice*, I thought, *at least not until it gets to know me.*

Witherer's box was tucked away in the lower-left corner of the trunk. Another simple box, it was inlaid with dual bars. It was an odd-looking wand with the power to age any living thing. Instead of the typical skull on a shaft, it was made from the petrified remains of a greenish-brown serpent. I was curious but had been afraid to touch it. What if it aged me? Lady Solendra would not be thrilled if my hair suddenly turned white. With just my fingertip, I tapped the body. Oddly, I felt nothing. I ran my finger along its scaly spine and still nothing. I picked it up for a closer examination. I did not react to it at all. Thinking it was dead, I placed it back in the box and set it next to Wrecker's box in order to store the wands conveniently together. As soon as the boxes touched, a violent spark flashed like lightning, causing me to jump. Two more sparks shot Wrecker's box clear out of the trunk. I saw Witherer shaking its head side-to-side in my mind.

I ran to Lord Whispa's book. Flicking through the pages, I scanned for the passage I was searching for, a passage I never understood before. I found it on page six twenty-two, and I read with great interest.

"'UU' one was a gift from my brothers," read the writing.

It wasn't two U's, it was a W, code for a wand. The inlay on Wrecker's box was not the letter "I," it was the number one. The dual bars on Witherer's box represented the number two.

"I created UU two," the writings continued. "UU two was based on the works of Lord Incara. Taking a hundred winters of prep and seal, I finally bound it to the other side this sun. It knows me. I am its father."

Lord Whispa, I thought, *you sneaky little cheat. You created a wand that likes necromancers. It just hates other wands or anything dark magic. That's how you managed to hold two wands at once. All this time you had everyone fooled. They thought you were so powerful. They were all impressed and it was just a trick. Wait, if Lord Whispa is its father, perhaps it sees me as its brother.* I saw Witherer nod in my mind.

"If you like killing demons," I said to it, "you're about to get your chance."

It nodded once more.

I put Banisher on my right and Witherer on my left. I slid a couple of poison-infused daggers into my belt, completing my armament.

"Well, my friend," I said to the helmet, "you and I haven't gotten to know each other either, but I need you now. I hope you can accept me as you did Lord Whispa."

I tucked the helm under my arm, threw a healing potion belt over my right shoulder, and a belt of poisons over my left. I had to be extra careful with the poisons. Until I was immune, these vials were as dangerous to me as they were to my enemies.

I proceeded to the barracks. Several men were quietly packing their belongings.

"Put your dressings back," I commanded.

They shot to attention. A couple were shivering and one pissed himself.

"No one is going anywhere," I continued.

A guardian can be especially intimidating to a deserter.

"Where is your commanding officer?" I asked as I confronted the soldier with the piss running down his leg.

He pointed to the back room. I stared each man down until his eyes dropped to the floor. Upon opening the backroom door, I found a captain, naked, sharpening his sword.

"Are you in command?"

"MY PRINCE!" He shot to his feet trying desperately to find his pants. "Yes, yes—Captain Deric in charge, sir."

"We have no majors or colonels?"

"Our major fled with the news. I haven't seen him since the announcement."

"Do you know that five of your men in the next room are preparing to do the same?"

"I'm not surprised. The men are scared. Most have never even seen a demon before, yet alone fought one."

"And what are you doing to stop the exodus?"

"Getting ready to fight with whoever is brave enough or dumb enough to stay."

"I see. And why are you staying?"

"They're fools. If Surdon falls, the demons will sweep through the other kingdoms. I have a woman and two daughters back home. I fight for them."

"Put your pants on and gather your men in the court. I'll give you exactly a twentieth sun to achieve this. Get going."

"Yes, my Prince."

I returned to the other room to see three of the men putting their things back. It appears I was more frightening than a demon. One was sitting on a bench weeping. The fifth was sitting on the floor, hands clutching his knees and rocking back and forth.

"Are you going to kill us?" one asked.

"I need you to listen to me closely. Necromancers are the most dangerous warriors to ever walk Atlantis. We have an army of them coming. All you should be worried about is what part of a demon's body you want to take home as a trophy."

The crying man wiped his face and said, "I heard they eat the fallen alive." That led to another burst of tears.

"You know what I think …"

I wanted to growl. Not a spell or an emotation, it was more of a trick of intimidation. I had never done it before, but I couldn't think of a better time to try. I emoted into my mouth; it was going to work.

"I think the demons should be scared of me."

My voice emanated with a low powerful hiss as the blue fog escaped my mouth like breath on a cold sun. I had to admit, that was awesome. I let my mana dissipate to restore my normal vocal tone.

"Stand up, soldier. You are a proud warrior of Surdon."

"I'm a coward. I am not worthy of that uniform."

"Why? Because you're scared? Bravery is not the absence of fear; it's doing it anyway. A soldier without fear takes too many risks. I would rather have smart soldiers than dead ones. Are you a smart soldier? Put on your uniform. Fight brave. Fight hard."

He looked me in the eye for the first time. The tears stopped.

"All you men, put on your uniforms and stand in formation with your brother warriors, where you deserve to be."

"YES, MY PRINCE!" they shouted in unison.

I entered the courtyard where the men were assembled. In their rush, not all were in uniform. Captain Deric greeted me.

"Report," I requested.

"We have six hundred and fifty men, give or take. One hundred and twenty-five archers, one hundred and fifty swordsmen, eighty horsemen, sixty barrage, and the rest are trainees, my Prince."

"MEN!" I shouted, pausing for dramatic effect. "I want you to close your eyes. Don't think about it, just do it. Now imagine your parents, your children, your girl, your friends all being chewed to pieces by demon-dogs. Really, see it. Hear their screams. Hear the unanswered pleas for help. See their blood as they are ripped to shreds. You are the ones that stand between them and that fate. We few have been given that honor. Wipe that vision clean. Now, imagine seeing their smiles as they greet the heroes of the battle of Surdon. Imagine you're one of those heroes. Your actions over the next few suns will create one of those two realities. Choose your actions as if their lives depend on it because they do. FIGHT BRAVE! FIGHT HARD!"

"FIGHT BRAVE! FIGHT HARD!" the men screamed in response.

"Now go. Sharpen your weapons and polish your armor for we will be victorious!"

"YEAH!"

"Major Deric—" I said.

"I'm sorry, my Prince, you misunderstood. I'm only a captain."

"I think I called it correctly, major. I need to speak with your lancers. Call them in."

"HORSEMEN, TO ME," he shouted as to be heard over the cheers.

They gathered in a circle around the major and me.

"I know that most of your mounts were sent to the trench," I began. "Some of you haven't ridden in a winter. That is why the next few suns of training are going to be crucial. I am opening the palace stables for your usage."

"Excuse me, my Lord," a sergeant interrupted. "Those are pleasure horses. What good are they going to be in battle?"

"Yes. You're right. Most of them are. That is why I am putting Lady Solendra in charge of your training."

They bursted into a clammer.

"You have to be kidding?" exclaimed one of the lancers. "You want us to take orders from a sorceress, a damn sorceress?"

Shouts of agreement echoed through the group. I prepared the growl and emoted with my eyes.

"You can either respect her or confront me," my voice echoed. "Which do you choose?"

They grew quiet as the blue steam from my mouth subsided.

"As of this sun, I have been bonded with Lady Solendra. She is now a princess of Surdon and you will treat her as such. You will refer to her as lady, your highness, or captain, and nothing else. She is one of the finest horsemen I have ever had the pleasure to know. Over the last four moons, she has whipped my sorry ass into shape. She has taught me how to move an animal in ways I didn't think were possible. If she can do that for me, she can help you. Report to her at the stables immediately. Is that clear?"

"YES, SIR!"

"Major, a moment. I need you to go with the lancers to the stables. I want you to make sure Lady Solendra's command gets off to a good start. Don't be afraid to kick some butt if needed. Plus, she doesn't know anything about this yet, so you'll have to inform her of my decision. You may have noticed I promoted her to captain and not major. You are still in overall command of the guard, but I want you to give her a free hand with the lancers. And after that, upgrade your uniform to display your new rank."

"Thank you, my Prince. I will try to be worthy of this honor."

"I know you will be."

Chapter #24

First Wave

I climbed the stairs to the ramparts and looked out toward the forest. Dark smoke from their fires rose over the canopy. The massive demon horde had crept through the rain-soaked fields giving us six suns to prepare. Still, we were barely ready. The trees hid their numbers, but their sounds hinted at thousands. I'm not sure which was thicker, the stone walls or the tension.

Lord Loter stepped up from behind.

"If I'm not mistaken," he said, "that's Lord Whispa's armor you're wearing."

"You are mistaken, my Lord," I retorted. "This is Guardian Timikia's armor."

He chuckled in response.

"I knew your mother lied to us. So, what do you think, kid?" he asked, looking across the cleared field.

"This is not good," I responded.

"That's a pretty accurate assessment."

"Do you think they'll strike tonight?" I asked.

"Hard to say. I think what we are looking at is the first wave. They might attack soon or wait for reinforcements. I don't see any siege weapons yet, but I do see keepers peeking out of the trees. That would mean scourges. We have to wait for them to make the first move. The waiting is the worst part. You should get some food and rest."

"I don't think I can eat."

"Force yourself. Once the action starts, it could be a long time before your next meal. Plus, I think I saw your lady chatting with some old friends of yours."

"Friends?"

"Yeah," he said with a grin, "I was surprised you had friends too.

Go get some rest, kid. You're going to need it."

After reaching the bottom of the steps, I scanned the preparation area until I spotted him just outside the mess tent.

"They'll let any bum into this war," I said, sneaking up from behind.

"PRINCEY!" Tomas threw his arms around me. "Look at you all armored up. If I didn't know better, I would think you knew what you were doing."

"Nice. Real nice. Are you a guardian yet?"

"Not yet. They promised if I survived this nonsense, they would promote me."

"How are the other idiots doing?"

"Ask them yourself. They're inside."

I found the whole gang in the mess tent, talking to Lady Solendra. I punched Pertwee in the arm.

"Hey, you chatting up my girl?"

"Timi! Damn good to see you, boy. How did a sad specimen like you land a beauty like this?"

"Dumb luck, I think."

"You got the dumb part right anyway."

"Pertwee, you never change."

"Would you really want me to? You don't mess with perfection. Lady Solendra has been telling us you inherited a bunch of Lord Whispa's stuff."

I held out my arms and turned full-circle twice, showing off my garb.

"Wow, that's good," said Flames. "It will be a long time before I can afford anything like that."

"Yeah, but I see you've donned guardian green," I replied.

"Pretty awesome, right? I got promoted a few moons after you left."

"Hey, Zip, you still hanging out with these losers?"

"Nah, it's just Tomas and me now. We adopted a couple of new-bies. They're more worthless than you were."

"So, you're the new Pertwee, huh?"

"That's not too hard. They're little shoes to fill," Zip joked.

"Hey!" barked Pertwee. "That might be true, but hey!"

"So, tell me, gang," I asked, "what lords have you been assigned to?"

"Tomas and I," Pertwee began, "were assigned to Lord Vicar."

"Vicar!" I said, "He's here?"

"Yeah. And still as big a hard ass as ever."

"Lord Poundra absorbed Zip and me," Flames chimed in.

"Oh," I replied, "so you two are guarding the trebuchets?"

"It a boring job, but somebody's got to do it."

"Speaking of jobs," Pertwee interjected, "we'd better get back on duty before lord hard ass turns us into skels. Catch you around, Timi."

"Us, too," Flames added. "Those pieces of wood aren't going to guard themselves."

"You five are close, aren't you," Lady Solendra said.

"I think I would have gone crazy at Nocmara if it wasn't for them. I love them like brothers."

"Seeing you together makes me miss my sisters."

"Maybe when all this is over, you can go visit them."

"Doubtful. After my outburst at Mother, I doubt I will ever see home again."

I reached out and squeezed her hand.

"I'm sorry I haven't had much time for you. Motivating troops is harder than I thought."

A gleam appeared in her eye.

"At least we had last night," she smiled.

That fond memory gave me joy.

"And we'll have many more nights. I promise."

"Prince Timikia," a young fledgling interrupted, "Lord Loter is requesting your presence at the wall."

"I'm coming with you," Lady Solendra said.

"I'd prefer if you'd portal someplace north. Someplace safe."

"You can't tell me what to do."

"I know, we've established that already. Come on."

The fledgling led us to Lord Loter. He looked more serious and stoic than usual.

"What's happened?" I asked, dreading the answer.

"Look at the four of them out there, seated on their mounts, waving a white flag. They want to talk."

"Is that a good thing or a bad thing?"

"It's a thing," Lord Loter said, handing me a spyglass. "Take a look at the one in the center. What does that look like to you?"

"Very tall. Thin. Gray skin. Damn, it's a mock."

"What's a mock?" Lady Solendra asked.

"A mock, my dear sorceress," Lord Loter explained, "is a very old, extremely rare class of demon. They have a special way of speaking that gets in your head. They can make you say and do things against your self-interest. They mock you. They can be extremely dangerous."

"Who are you going to send out there?" I inquired.

"Lord Mar, myself, and you."

"Me! Why me?"

"We need a royal. The blackheart on the right looks like a duke. Royalty expects royalty. Would you prefer I bring your mother?"

"But they have a mock. I don't have the mental fortitude that you and Lord Mar have."

"Mocks are a danger to everyone, including lords. However, they are most dangerous when they use their abilities against one person. It's difficult for them to control a group. If there are four of us, we should be able to hold him off. We'll only be out there for a little while. Just remember what it took to defeat the room and you'll be fine. Guardian Timikia, who would you select as our fourth emissary?"

"That would be me," Lady Solendra chimed in.

"Like hell, it will!" I spouted.

"You can't tell me—"

"I know. I know. I know. We've established that already. But I'm putting my foot down this time. There is no good reason for you to be out there."

"Yes, there is. For all I know, I may already be excommunicated from the Coven by now, but the demons don't know that. Seeing me out there might make them think twice. If they think the Sorceri are manning the walls too, they might withdraw."

"No. No. No. I'm not about to let—"

"The Princess makes a good point," Lord Loter observed. "But nothing in Sorceri training has prepared you for a mock, my good Lady. We don't need you to talk, we just need your presence. I'll do the talking for everyone. But if the mock speaks, I'll need you to chant the same phrase in your mind over and over and over again. Something like, 'the dog barks loudly.' If you keep your mind focused on that, you might be able to drown out his words."

"I don't like this," I said.

"We all have to play our part," Lord Loter replied. "This might be the single most important thing that Lady Solendra can do right now. Riding out to meet our enemy, within an arrow shot of both sides takes nerves of steel. I commend you, my Lady. Your bravery is a credit to your clan."

The four of us rode out to meet them. As we grew closer, there was indeed a blackheart duke, a blackheart general, a heavily armored warrior of an unknown clan, and, of course, the mock. The two blackhearts were hooded to protect their pale skin from the light. We stopped about fifteen horse lengths apart.

It was the first time I had seen a blackheart close up. The drawings at Nocmara did not do them justice. Their hands were gigantic, easily twice the size of mine. The skin on their fingers was rough and scarred from winters of working in the mines. The second thumb didn't attach to the bottom of their hands as I had imagined; they protruded from the bottom of their forearm and were about three times the length of a normal thumb, almost like a claw. I thought Solendra's black hair was the darkest I had ever seen, but the blackheart's hair was so void of color it resembled a hole in the world. The only other time I had seen something that dark was on the other side. I could just make out their pale white eyes that seemed to glow from under their hoods. They gave me the creeps.

Creepier still was the mock. Mocks are so rare there were no drawings of them at Nocmara. What I knew of them I gathered from descriptions written long ago. The deep wrinkles of gray flesh on his forehead hung down like a hound dog. His furrowed eyebrows obscured his eyes. I had read they were groomed that way on purpose to mask their expressions. His small mouth was framed by sparse lips. He had a long chin that almost came to a point. All that was wrapped in a colorless gray pallor that made you wonder if he was alive.

The warrior wore smooth and featureless armor. From a distance, his armor appeared to be made of gold. Up close the metal was a brass compound, probably something only the blackhearts knew how to make. His entire face was covered by a massive helmet with two small eye silts that were nothing but black at this distance. He was cloaked in a long black cape that he held tightly to his sides keeping his weapons a mystery. The two blackhearts and the mock were adorned ornately, but the warrior's armor was about function. This man, if he was a man, was a killer.

"We're here," Lord Loter said. "Talk."

"Who's ssss … are you sss …"

The mock's voice echoed in my head like a scream in a deep canyon. There was a tingle at the base of my spine. I saw Lady

Solendra's eyes widen.

"I am Lord Loter, head military officer of the Brotherhood. This is Lord Mar, key diplomat of the Brotherhood. To my left, Guardian Timikia, crown prince of Surdon and Lady Solendra, mage of the Sorceri."

"Sorceri ... hmmm ... we sss," he said intently staring at Solendra, "are Duke Blacar and Tur Micar of the Deep, Black Pit. I am Sssesssao of the Speakers. And my gold-armored friend here is the General."

"The General has no name?" Lord Loter inquired.

"He ssss no need of a name."

Solendra stiffened. She closed her eyes and bit her lip.

"What sss ... wrong ssss my Lady sss you look ssss troubled sss ... problems at home sss ... or maybe with Mother sss ..."

Her hand shook as she reached for her wand. I had had enough. I drew both my wands and emoted. The sight of a necromancer baring two wands scared the mock white. His horse reared and fell back. The blackheart general and Lord Mar drew their weapons.

"WHOA! WHOA!" shouted the Duke. "Everyone, calm down. We didn't come out here to fight."

"If that mock," I spat, "so much as utters another syllable, you won't have a choice. I'll take his head off and feed it to my dogs."

"Very well," replied the Duke. "Everyone, relax. Put your weapons away. I'll speak for our side. I have come here to offer you terms."

"Terms?" said Lord Loter.

"Terms of surrender. You can't win. Open your gates. Surrender the city and we'll allow your people to leave in peace."

"And then what?"

"We'll be content with Palace City. We will stop our attack."

"And, if we don't trust you?"

"Does it matter? One way or the other the city will fall to us. You can die defending it—or not."

"We need time to consider your proposal."

"Of course, you can have until sunup tomorrow. I will need your answer by then."

Lord Loter turned his horse and our party withdrew.

"Are you crazy?" I spat. "This is my mother's city. You can't just give it away."

"I have no intention of doing so. That was the dance, kid. The demons need a bit more time to set up their attack. This was only a ploy to try and prevent us from attacking first. We don't have the troops to do that, but that is information they don't possess. They have no intention of stopping with Palace City. They want the entire Southern Realm. I said what I had to say to get us off the field in one piece. They'll probably attack in the morning."

"Don't blackhearts attack at night?"

"That's one of the reasons I came out here. I wanted to get a closer look. The trees are lined with scourges. The blackhearts are probably still moving their siege weapons through the dense trees. Scourges fight in the light of the sun. They'll attack at first light, and there's going to be a lot of them."

As we passed through the gates, Lady Solendra fell off her horse. Two soldiers caught her before she hit the ground. I leapt down and ran to her side.

"He's in my head," she panted. "I can feel him in my head."

I looked up to Lord Loter for assistance.

"It'll pass," he said. "Find her a bed. Let her get some rest. It'll pass."

She was still wobbly as I helped her to her feet. With a soldier's aid, I took her to the rest tent and laid her down. She clutched my hand to her breast.

"He made me want to kill you. I really wanted to." She burst into tears.

"He's gone now. He can't hurt you anymore. Everything is going to be all right."

My mother crashed into the tent. She knelt beside the cot and took Lady Solendra's hand.

"I came as soon as I heard. Are you all right?"

"I will be, my Queen. I will be."

"Call me, Mother."

Lord Mar entered the tent.

"Prince Timikia," he commanded, "we need you at the wall."

"No. I'm staying here."

"Your men need you at the wall."

"They'll be fine without me."

Lord Mar put his hand on my shoulder.

"No, they won't. They need to see you standing tall. They're scared, but they'll be empowered by your bravery. They are watching your every move. You're going to have to be stronger than you ever thought possible."

"Go on, my son," Mother implored. "I'll stay with her. I won't leave her side."

Walking out was the hardest thing I've ever done.

Chapter #25

The First Goodbye

We were all waiting for the briefing to start. Lord Loter's outline was silhouetted against the firelight as I sat with my gang of friends. There was no joking with each other this night. Sleep had escaped all of us as we prepared for the dawn. Lord Mar and Lord Loter were conferring with one another when Lady Solendra arrived. Pertwee slid over to make room for her next to me.

"How are you feeling?" I inquired.

"Much better," my consort replied.

"Do you still want to kill me?"

"Sometimes, but not because of the mock."

She smiled and squeezed my hand.

"I'm sorry to tell you this," I said, "but this briefing is only for necromancers."

"I know."

She didn't leave.

"Good morning, my brothers," Lord Loter began. "I'm sure you all know the situation by now. I have called this briefing because it will be light soon, and I need you to understand the plan. The Council and Major Duric have agreed on a defensive strategy. We're going to send the golems into the field to meet the scourges head-on. Since the demons don't care if they kill scourges, our golems will most likely be showered with arrows. Under a barrage like that, they won't last long. As soon as the scourges start to fall, I need you to skel them up as quickly as you can. We need to turn our numbers and the tides of battle as soon as possible. Remember to call out your reanimation targets. I don't need mana fights over corpses. This will leave most of you drained, so save your mana and let the archers pick off the survivors. Have your wands at the ready in case any of them breach the wall.

Bring up your golems and have them ready to go. Good hunting, my brothers. FIGHT BRAVE. FIGHT HARD."

"FIGHT BRAVE! FIGHT HARD!" the group chanted back.

"I feel like my Coven education failed me," Solendra said. "I'm embarrassed how little I know about demons."

"Don't be embarrassed," I replied. "It's been a long time since the Sorceri fought the demons. The Coven grew complacent for the most part. The Brotherhood had major battles with them less than twenty winters ago. They are a much bigger threat to us."

"So, what's a scourge?" she whispered.

"Foul, nasty little things, about the height of your mid-thigh. They're a greenish-gray color with large bulging eyes and completely hairless. They're fairly easy to kill, especially if you strike the neck. Their heads are big compared to their bodies, so it's simple to snap their spines like twigs."

"They don't sound that bad."

"One-on-one they're not, but there's never just one. They come at you in packs and have no fear. You could kill a thousand and they would keep coming. They are capable of using simple weapons, like a dagger, but prefer their razor-sharp teeth and claws. Their major weakness is their stupidity, and they have no tactics other than a hell-bent rush. Sometimes, they will get distracted in battle and stop to feed on the carnage, even their own kind."

"Being that dumb and small, how are they going to get over the wall?"

"A scourge could climb up a wet piece of glass. They could scale our stone walls with ease. Any chance you would reconsider and return to the relative safety of the palace."

"Nope."

"I didn't think so."

Golems of all four types began to appear in the court. The simple mud golems were the most prevalent. This made sense due to the large number of fledglings and guardians among the brothers. Raised from small animals, the more complex blood golems grossed out Lady Solendra. This was understandable with their blood coursing through their veins beneath almost transparent skin. There were far fewer iron golems than I hoped. I was one of the few necromancers that ever produced one as a fledgling. The technically difficult fire golems were in short supply. Still, it seemed like it would be enough to fend off this first wave.

The sun peeked over the trees and cast long, ominous shadows across the battlefield. That's when it started—the low, violent chirping of the scourges. The sound echoed against the city walls until it was hard to hear yourself think. Like a disgusting boil ready to pop, the scourges swelled out from the forest with their keepers whipping them into a loose formation.

Lord Loter motioned the golems to the gate. My golem, Victus, and I shared a silent moment before I sent him to join the other minions.

Lady Solendra and I made our way up to the ramparts. I felt the weight of the soldiers' eyes upon me as I ascended the last step.

"THIS SUN, MEN," I shouted, wanting to be heard by as many as possible, "WE FIGHT FOR OUR LAND, OUR KINGDOM, OUR FAMILIES, AND OURSELVES. AND KNOW THIS—IF YOU FALL THIS SUN—I WILL FALL WITH YOU. I WILL STAND BY YOUR SIDE UNTIL THE END. BUT—SINCE I DO NOT INTEND TO FALL—NEITHER WILL YOU! FIGHT BRAVE! FIGHT HARD!"

I drew both my wands and emoted into the sky.

"Two wands," I heard a soldier whisper.

"It's like the return of Lord Whispa," said another.

"He's better than his father," expressed a third.

And then it began.

"TIM-I-KIA! TIM-I-KIA! TIM-I-KIA!"

The chanting went on and on. Lord Loter joined me at the wall.

"A bit overdramatic," he began, "but I liked it."

"You're not impressed with two wands?"

"What? That you can hold Witherer? Keep dreaming, kid."

"Oh, so you know the secret."

"Of course, I do."

"Are you going to expose me for the fraud I am?"

With a frown, he said, "You never have understood me, have you? If it's good for the Brotherhood, it's good for us all. It's good for me. There is a valuable lesson for you in this. It's not always about what you can do, it's about what people think you can do. Now, get your over-inflated self in check and focus on the battle."

The golems roared out of the gate and charged the scourge mass. The keepers held the monstrous creatures back.

"What are they waiting for?" questioned Lord Loter. "Why aren't the scourges attacking?"

The scourges parted up the middle to make way for a single gold-en-clad figure. It was the General. His armor sparkled in the morning's light. He stood calmly as the bickering horde howled behind him.

"LORDS! HAVE YOUR FIRE GOLEMS LEAD," Lord Loter commanded. "FOCUS ON THE GENERAL!"

Seven powerful, burning creatures charged the demons' golden leader. He remained still and confident. With a vicious wave of the General's arm, the flaming golems disappeared in puffs of black smoke before our eyes.

"WHAT?" Lord Loter erupted.

It can't be, I thought. *It can't be true.*

Another wave of his arm and the mud golems withered back into the earth. With another wave of his hand, the blood golems popped in crimson explosions and the iron golems melted down into molten pools of steel. When the last of the golems had fallen, the General gazed at us in defiance and waved his mass forward. The gray wave rushed across the field unopposed.

"Do you still have that purple wall in your back pocket?" Lord Loter asked.

"Yeah, but to make one big enough would take everything I've got. I wouldn't have the strength to move it around."

"How do you move it around?"

"Emotation," I replied.

"Emotation, huh? We'd have to be close to move it. I'll worry about moving it around. You bring up as large a wall as possible."

"You're going out there? That's suicide."

"That's what heroes do, kid. Want to be a hero? Get that wall up and keep it up as long as you can."

"LORD VICAR!" Lord Loter barked. "You and your team join me at the gate."

"Solendra," I said, "no matter what happens, I need you to keep me standing. I need to be able to see over the battlements."

Lady Solendra agreed and commanded a soldier to help her with the task.

Lord Loter, Lord Vicar, and a small group of guardians and fledglings dashed out the gate. The group included my friends, Pertwee and Tomas. Straight toward the horde they ran.

Quivering, I drew the entirety of my mana into my arms. It burned worse than my first wand. With a scream from hell, I blasted emotation down onto the battlefield. The purple death wall exploded up from the mud, shielding my friends from the horde. My skin felt like it was being ripped away with vibrations heaving off my body. It was all Lady Solendra and the soldier could do to hang onto me. Several others soldiers ran to assist them.

The advancing necromancers lit up the morning dew in a blue mist and pushed the wall forward. Too stupid to avoid it, many of the beasts ran straight into the wall of death. A violent popping noise echoed across the field as each one was sucked in. Lord Loter directed the path to absorb as many of the creatures as possible. I fought to stop myself from blacking out. My body convulsed as my mana ran dry. The wall dissolved into a purple fog and the remaining scourges poured through the haze.

Lord Loter sounded the retreat and the team raced back toward the gates, with the horde hot on their heels.

"ARCHERS," roared Major Deric, "COVER THEIR ESCAPE!"

A shower of arrows flew from the battlements and dropped on the gray bodies below. Still, they came.

"COME ON! COME ON!" encouraged the soldiers waiting to close the gates.

Tomas stumbled as his boot sank into the mud. He emoted and bounced two attacking beasts away from him. Lord Loter and Pertwee turned to help as three scourges pounced on Tomas. I could hear his screams from my perch. Lord Loter blew back a pack of them as Pertwee struck the ones latched on to my friend. He struggled to free Tomas's foot. The scourges surrounded the three of them. Lord Loter encased the group in a protective bone cage the largest I had ever seen. Scourges leapt onto the bones. Feeling helpless, I watched as the little monsters tried to scratch and claw their way in.

A group of scourges reached the base of the wall and started their ascent. My soldiers poured boiling water on them and threw boulders, but they kept coming. A group of twenty bounded over the battlements and overwhelmed two nearby archers. The soldiers dropped me to the floor. Drawing their swords, they positioned themselves to defend me. I was so weak I couldn't lift my head. Lady Solendra pushed her way past the two soldiers. Her arm and wand lit up with a bright yellow glow. A powerful flame shot from her wand setting the closest ones ablaze. She drove them back over the wall, many falling to their deaths. A straggler scampered around her flames and leapt for her throat. With an accurate cut, a soldier removed its head, sending it careening to the court below. Solendra burned several more off the wall.

It was over. The archers picked off the few remaining scourges that fought on, but they had been decimated.

"Get me to the wall," I begged.

Lady Solendra ran to my aid. She directed the soldiers to help me. They propped me up on the battlements. Lord Loter and Pertwee were dragging a limp Tomas behind them.

"Take me to the gate—hurry!" I cried.

I struggled to move my legs. We arrived at the gate as the three came in. Tomas was covered in blood.

"Come on, Tomas," Pertwee cried. "Come on, wake up!"

"Don't bother," said Lord Loter. "He's gone."

"Wait," I interjected. "I have healing potions. We can save him."

"I already gave him two," Lord Loter said. "We didn't get to him in time."

"NO! NO! NO!" screamed Pertwee.

Lord Loter crossed his arms over his own chest. "Until we meet on the other side."

It was the traditional necromancer's honor of passage. I had never heard of it being done for a fledgling before.

"My Lady," I requested, "please help me cross my arms. I'm too weak to do it myself."

"Don't you dare!" Mar exploded at me as he stepped up from behind.

"I know he was just a fledgling, but I—"

"Yes, he was a fledgling and a hero. He deserves to be honored, but not by you!"

"What are you talking about?"

"You helped him cheat the room. He shouldn't have been a fledgling. This man is dead because of you, Timikia."

"That's enough," said Lord Loter.

"Is it? I'm tired of the other Council members covering for Timikia's mistakes," said Lord Mar.

With a sneer, he stormed off.

"What an ass!" countered Lady Solendra, holding me tighter.

"Yeah, but he's right," I said.

"Tomas was your friend. You wouldn't have done anything to hurt him." Solendra's feminine voice was of no comfort to me at that moment.

"And yet, I did."

"Say it," Lady Solendra said as she folded my arms across my chest.

"Until we meet on the other side, my friend. Until then," I whispered, holding back my tears.

Chapter #26

What's the Truth?

The light crept through my eyelids like a slithering snake. Slow shallow breaths reminded me I was still alive. Peering up, an angel stood over me.

"Good morning, sleepyhead," said Lady Solendra. "Welcome back to this side my Prince."

A strong hand jerked my head around, and then stubby fingers pried my left eye open.

"Look side-to-side quickly," a low voice commanded.

"Wha … who are you?"

"Just do it!" he barked. "That's looking better. You'll live."

"Who are you, again?"

"Lord Merindin."

"The famous HEALER?"

"Yes. Consider yourself lucky I was around."

"It's with great pleasure I am in your presence, my Lord."

"Didn't anyone tell you? You can't rip all of your mana away in one shot like that? You could have shattered the bones in your arms—or worse. How long have you been greening?"

"Almost three moons."

"When was your last dose?"

"Ah … five or six suns ago … maybe seven. I'm not sure."

"That explains your clammy skin. Once you start you have to keep going."

"I know."

"DO YOU?"

"If you weren't aware, my Lord … I've been kind of busy."

"It doesn't matter. If the dries set in, you'll be out of commission for a moon or two and have to start all over again. Let me see the poison you're using."

"Um … my bottle is in my lab, but it's similar to the mixture on my belt there."

Lord Merindin examined the contents of the small glass flask.

"YOU made this?" he said.

"No. It's part of Lord Whispa's old stock."

"How much have you been using?"

"I'm embarrassed to admit it. I've only been able to do two drops so far. I can barely handle that."

"TWO DROPS! It's amazing, you're not dead. I can't even see through this stuff. It has to be nine-tenths pure at least. Lord Loter told me you were an idiot and now I believe him. What kind of guardians are Nocmara promoting these suns? Here, take this bottle. It's properly diluted. Start with four drops and make sure you dose, THIS SUN!"

I finally got to meet one of my heroes and he rips me to pieces.

"Can I buy Lord Whispa's bottle off you?" he asked. "I'd like to do some testing because it's an unusual color."

"Take two of them," I replied. "Consider it payment for your kindness and skill."

"Thanks. And what are you going to do this sun?"

"Greening."

"Damn straight. I gave you a small dose while you were out. That should get you balanced by mid-sun, but it won't hold you for long."

With a nod, he left.

"You look like you haven't slept all night," I said, turning my attention to Solendra.

"I didn't. You have no idea how close we came to losing you. I've been by your side this whole time. Your mother, too. She left a little bit ago. Something about trouble at the portal. Don't you do this to me again," she added, throwing her arms around me.

"I'll try not to."

"Someone wants to speak with you. Are you up to it?"

"Yeah. Let them in," I said, sitting up in my cot.

"I'll go get him."

Solendra opened the tent flap and in stepped Lord Loter. Lady Solendra stepped out but left the flap open. She pretended not to listen in, but I knew better.

"You're looking better," Lord Loter said. "When you collapsed, we feared the worst."

"I'm sorry."

"Sorry? For what? Sorry, you passed out?"

"No, not that. If I had given you the death wall spell when you asked, Tomas would still be alive."

"You don't know that."

"Yes, I do. With your massive mana, you'd have generated a huge wall and held it longer. I let down everyone. I failed my kingdom, my people, and especially Tomas."

"You have to let that go, kid. If you don't, it will eat you alive. See that beautiful young woman, the one to whom you've paired yourself? You'll watch her grow old and die. If you have children, you'll watch them grow old and die. If you start another family, you will watch that brood grow old and die. People think a long life is a gift; it's not. It's the necromancer's curse. Tomas was the first to die in this exchange, but he won't be the last. You're going to have to learn to accept that which you cannot change. If you want to be a lord, you'll witness the death of everyone you care about. I have lost many friends in battle. I raised and lost three families. I'm alone now, but to be honest with you, kid—regret is not a good way to live. Be happy you knew Tomas. You may yet meet him on the other side. I know it's hard, but you have to let go. There is only so much heartbreak a man can withstand. It almost destroyed your father."

I had definitely heard better pep talks.

"How do I get the memory of my blood-soaked friend out of my mind?"

"Can you stand?" Lord Loter asked. "There is something I need you to see."

With his help, we walked out of the healer's tent. Hundreds of soldiers, fledglings, guardians, and Surdon citizens were sitting around the tent. Upon spotting me, a few stood and applauded. They were joined by more and then the cheering started.

"TIM-I-KIA! TIM-I-KIA! TIM-I-KIA!"

"They've been sitting here all night," said Lord Loter. "We lost six soldiers and a fledgling last sun. We destroyed thousands of them. The demons are off licking their wounds. I have never been part of a greater one-sided victory. It's not over yet, but for this sun, you're their hero. Many of these people saw the sunrise because of you. They don't think you should be sorry and neither do I. You put your life on the line to save your people because that's what heroes do. They say a lord is worth a hundred men on the battlefield. A hero is worth a thousand. Look at these people. They're motivated and ready to fight.

You did that. What you did last sun may save your kingdom. When bad thoughts start to flood your mind, focus on this moment, on these people."

"TIM-I-KIA! TIM-I-KIA! TIM-I-KIA!"

A chanting Lady Solendra took my hand and raised it above my head. The crowd went crazy. But still, I couldn't get Tomas's smiling face out of my thoughts.

"Princess Solendra," said an out-of-breath page. "Queen Lika requests your presence at the portal. The Queen requested your presence too, my Prince, if you are strong enough."

"What is this regarding?" asked Lady Solendra.

"There has been a request to unlock the portal. A request from the Sorceri."

"Get armored up, kid," Lord Loter suggested. "I don't trust the Coven. I don't trust their motives. Plus, the Sorceri's portal could have been overrun by the demons. The horde could be masquerading as the Sorceri. We have to make a show of force, so I'll round up a few squads of brothers. Lady Solendra, head over and scout things out. I'll look after the Prince. I think the Queen wants the unlocking of the path to be your call. If anything seems off, even a little bit, don't clear the portal."

"With the way I'm feeling, I wouldn't be much good in a fight," I said to him.

"Even after all the cheering, you still don't get it," he replied. "You, standing here, all armored up, is enough. Let's get you looking like a proper warrior. I'll help you."

In my weakened state, walking in full armor was a major chore. By the time we arrived at the portal square, a sizeable war party had surrounded it. Mother was in serious consultation with Lady Solendra.

"Can you catch me up?" I asked.

"The portal has been frantically flashing all morning," Mother explained. "The message is in code."

"It's a Sorceri code," Lady Solendra added, "but it's an old code that hasn't been used in a very long time."

"So, it's a fake?" I inquired.

"Or someone that wants to keep their transport a secret," Lady Solendra said.

"I don't like it," Mother stated. "Son, what do you think?"

"We need all the help we can get. If there's any chance of assistance, we have to risk it."

"All right," Mother relented. "Lord Loter, we are activating the portal. Prepare your forces."

Necromancers drew their wands. Soldiers armed themselves. If trouble emerged from the blue haze, we'd only have moments to drive them back. Through the thick tension, I noticed a couple of guardians with weapons pointed at my lady. In bad times, trust is not easily earned.

The portal flashed and out stepped a single sorceress. Her battle suit was similar to my Lady's except for a gold strip running the length of her arms. With long golden hair and a porcelain complexion, she stood fearless despite the many well-armed adversaries.

Lady Solendra ascended the four steps to confront her.

"What the hell are you doing here?" she asked.

"Is that any way to greet your sister?"

"If you've come to take me back, I'm not going."

"I know. You're stubborn to the core. We've come here—"

"We?"

The sorceress tapped the portal. Her actions put every necromancer on edge. Out of the blue haze stepped three more Sorceri. One had flaming red hair and freckles. Another was dark-skinned with a massive mane of black curly hair. The third was a young girl of twelve or thirteen winters with pale green eyes and wavy brown hair.

"We've come here to look after our sister. Somebody has to."

A smile burst across Lady Solendra's face as she embraced the golden-striped eldest. Lord Loter waved off his forces.

"My Prince, this is Meca, my second sister, and Thesca, my third sister," she said pointing to the redhead, "and Tamarica, my fourth sister. And this little one is Persa, who shouldn't be here."

"We tried to leave her at home," Meca said, "but she's as stubborn as you are."

"My lovely sisters, this is Prince Timikia."

"Oh," Meca began, "so this is the necro that twisted your brain around, the one you threw your life away for."

"NO! This is the man I'm starting my new life with."

"Whatever. Just tell him to stay out of our way when the fighting starts."

"Tell him yourself. He's standing right here."

Meca glanced at me out of the corner of her eye and smirked.

Trying to lighten the mood, Lady Solendra commented, "You got your stripe. Level nine. Wow."

"Yeah. I was adorned last moon. I finally passed all my wind tests."

"Where is Yeresta?"

"Back with Mother and little Meosa. Our eldest sister has chosen to stay behind. We had to bribe the portal guards to turn a blind eye. Mother doesn't know we're here. We've been waiting all morning for these idiots to open the portal. We're starved. Anything worth eating in this dump?"

"There is a mess tent on the other side of those buildings," I said.

"Great. Now if you can get this riff-raff out of our way we can get some chow. Come, ladies."

The four sisters pushed their way through a crowd of soldiers as if they owned the place.

"Was I that obnoxious when I first arrived?" Lady Solendra asked.

"Um … pretty much," I replied.

"How did you refrain from killing me?"

"Probably 'cause, I don't think I could have. I've seen you fight."

With a grin, she squeezed my hand.

"I need to talk with Mother," I said. "Why don't you join your sisters and I'll catch up with you tonight."

"Are you poisoning again? I've never heard it referred to as greening before."

"The older lords call it that. It makes it sound less painful."

"Well, be more careful in the future. Almost losing you once is enough."

After squeezing my hand again, she ran off.

"Mother, we need to talk. Alone."

"Of course. Let's go to my council chambers."

Upon arriving we sat in "The Chairs"—two plush seats that were reserved for Queen Lika's most trusted advisors. It was the first time I had been invited to sit there.

"The sun Father died," I began, "did you see him die?"

"That's a strange question. Of course, I did."

"No. I mean did you actually see him take his last breath?"

"Well, not exactly. The demons were closing in and he implored me and Lord Whispa to flee."

"Then, you're not positive he's dead."

"He was completely out of poison and mana. He could barely

breathe and the demons were rushing in. No one could have survived that, not even your father. What's this all about?"

"Lord Loter and I have been trying to classify the demons' new general. The one in the gold armor. We've seen him up close and he's not a blackheart. He doesn't have a tail so that limits the number of species he could be. He's too tall to be a frek, so that only leaves cons. Who's ever heard of a con being a general or a soldier. It's not in their nature."

"What does any of this have to do with your father?"

"At the beginning of the battle, the General zapped hundreds of golems back to the other side in a flash. That's a release spell. Father was the only necromancer to ever figure out that spell."

"If you think for a moment that thing out there is the great Lord Timicus, your father, the man I loved, then you're crazy! How dare you dishonor his memory."

"Lord Whispa has scoured the other side looking for him. He has found no trace. It could be because he is not there. He is here, waiting in the trees to pounce."

Mother started panting. "No. No. That can't be. Maybe the demons figured out the spell too. After all, they created the dark magic in the first place."

"And then they lost it. There hasn't been a dark magic-wielding demon in a thousand winters. Now there is. And, one with a release spell no less."

"I think you are letting your imagination get the better of you."

"Perhaps. But, if it is Lord Timicus, his powers have seriously grown. Lord Whispa told me that Father could only bring down one minion at a time. The General mowed them down like wheat in a field. He didn't even look tired afterward. If it's him—he would be our greatest threat."

Chapter #27

Speaking of the Dead

My lab was quiet, a place of loneliness. There was an emptiness to it that only a necromancer could understand. So much of what we do, we do solo. Lord Loter's words haunted me. It was the first time in winters I doubted my resolve to become a lord.

Carefully, I poured four drops into my palm. The color was muted compared to Lord Whispa's vibrant green fluid. If Lord Merindin hadn't pointed it out, I may not have noticed. Licking my palm, I began dosing. The pain swelled behind my eyes. I hated when the poison manifested itself in that manner. I could deal with the nausea, the nose bleeds, the shaking, but the head pounding was the worst. I focused on rechanneling the pain into sensation.

No, I thought. *Let the pain come. I need it. I need him.*

Waves of pain rippled down my face into my jaw, but it wasn't enough to create the desired affect. I drew Banisher.

"Come on monkey skull, do your thing," I said out loud while tucking the boney head behind my knee.

Like a swarm of fire ants, the pain spread up my thigh. My sight grew dark as reality faded. Then came the voices. It was my fourth trip beyond the barrier and still the crushing noise was difficult to endure.

"Where are you? Come on Lord Whispa, I need you!"

I floated aimlessly through the wisps as if bobbing on the sea. I was chilled to the core whenever they swept through me. Something seemed different. Something seemed off. A grasp of freezing fingers spun me around pushing me into the darkness of the in-between.

All was still. Into the darkness, a single wisp emerged. The faint outline of Lord Whispa's face floated in the center of the haze.

"It is good to see you, Timikia. Back so soon?"

"Good to see you, my friend."

"Things are not good here," Lord Whispa expressed. "Souls have been pouring in at an alarming rate. I have to assume most of Atlantis is at war."

"Yes. And Palace City is under siege."

"By whom?"

"The demons. They have a new general that wields the dark arts. He may have unified the tribes, giving them a new sense of purpose. They're attacking on multiple fronts simultaneously. And—I'm afraid their General might be Lord Timicus."

"What? Why do you think this?"

"He has a release spell. I saw him release a swarm of golems in ten breaths."

"Oh my! That's not good!"

"Is there a way I can test my theory?"

"Yes. Attack him with your golem," said Lord Whispa.

"I can't do that. Ever since the General cast his release spell, I can no longer communicate with my golem spirit. It's like he's gone. Others have experienced the same problem with their golems."

"He's not gone. He's ignoring you. He doesn't want to fight for you anymore."

"Why? He was a great warrior. I thought the two of us were friends?" I said.

"Let me explain. When you create a golem, a bond is formed between the two of you. When you release your golem, it's like saying goodbye, a painless process. But, when he is forced out by a rival, the bond you shared is shattered. The spirit unnaturally returns to the other side. It is a painful experience for him."

"Well, that's the end of that. No spirit. No golem."

"There's one major flaw in the release spell your father created. A spirit can be prepared to resist the magic. A soul imbued with this ability can stay planted on the life side."

"That's great. Tell me the secret and I can share it with—"

"It doesn't work that way. The spirit has to be prepared on the death side of the barrier. It took me winters to create a single one. His name is Karoc. In life, he was an armored rider for the Norsemen. I will link you to him. When Karoc attacks, the General will try to release him—and if he can't—he's your father."

"How could that possibly be? I can't wrap my head around my father leading the horde?"

"Have you seen any mocks?"

"Yes. One."

"Where there's one, there's probably more. The thought is too horrible to imagine," said Lord Whispa.

"What thought?"

"Thousands of winters ago, when mocks were more common, occasionally a lord would be captured. The mocks would chatter at them nonstop for winters—a horror I can't even comprehend. Eventually, the necromancer would snap. It was a fate so horrible that most lords would end themselves to avoid capture. The Brotherhood teamed up with the Druid Hive and hunted down the mocks. They drove them into extinction—or so they thought. If this is true, I cry for my old friend."

"I'll look for an opportunity, but I doubt if a single golem could get close enough."

"Go to my laboratory and find Witherer. It will be a great aid in battle. But before you do, I need to share a secret about that wand."

"I already know. You're a little sneak."

"Do you think less of me?"

"I never have and I never will. You will forever be my mentor, my friend, and—a father."

"I am being pulled back. I have to go. Fight brave. Fight hard."

The cold stone floor of the lab came back into focus.

Chapter #28

Sisterhood

"This place smells," Meca complained.

"It's not so bad once you get used to it," I replied.

"And this food is garbage. Solendra, how do you tolerate being here?"

"This food was rushed in for the troops. It's not my normal fare."

"What's he like?" questioned Thesca.

"Who? The Prince?" I asked.

"Yes. How horrible is he?"

"Actually … he's brave … kind … caring. He's a good man."

"It sounds like you like him or something," said Tamarica, with a spiteful tone.

"I do."

"That's just sick," Meca spouted.

"I think he's cute," Persa said in a shy little voice.

"Ewww!" my sisters groaned.

"Persa, just eat your slop," Meca ordered.

"But he is cute," Persa added.

"You're too young to know better," Meca said. "When you're older, you'll realize how disgusting he is. They haven't forced you to kiss him or anything like that, have they?"

"No," I replied. "They haven't forced me."

"At least that's something."

"I kiss him because I want to."

"Ewww!" everyone but Persa said in unison.

"How could Mother leave you in such a place. What have they done to your mind?"

"What have they done? They've opened my mind to the truth."

"And what truth is that?"

"Necromancers aren't monsters. They're people, just like us. They learn. They struggle. They build. They fight. And for the lucky ones—they love."

"By the gods," Tamarica griped, "she's in love with the creepy necro."

"I am. If you can't handle that—if you can't accept that—if you don't want to call me sister anymore, I'll understand."

They all grew quiet.

"I still think he's cute," Persa said.

We all laughed.

"All right. All right," said Meca. "You're in love, and I guess I can handle that. It could be worse. It could be a demon or a horse or something. But you have no idea what this is doing to Mother."

"She doesn't care," I retorted. "Everyone knows I'm the disappointment, her disposable daughter."

"You wouldn't say that if you could see her. She's a wreck."

"She left me here easy enough. She didn't even say goodbye."

"Mother has been painted into a corner. The Coven labeled you a traitor. That might be our fate too now that we chose to come here. Mother may be the High Mage, but she's not in charge. Her title hinges on a thread. If she dares cross the Coven, they'll take away her fourth stripe and maybe even her third."

"Her precious stripes are worth more than me. I get it."

"No, Solendra," Meca said, "I don't think you do."

"Then, enlighten me."

"It's time you knew the truth," Meca said. "What do you know about your father?"

"Yes. Yes. The Grand Duke of Paraguew, Lord Admiral of the Western Fleet—big deal. He couldn't even be bothered to visit me."

"No," Meca said, "he is not your father. That's the lie Mother told the Coven to protect you."

"Huh?" said Thesca.

Tamarica and Persa looked confused.

"We are all outlaws now," Meca continued, "so you might as well know. Your true father was a necro lord."

"NO WAY!" Persa spouted.

"Yes, little sister, it's true. Until now, only Yeresta and I knew about this. The Coven sometimes hires necros to do their dirty work. It's their nasty little secret. Mother met Solendra's father on a quest to destroy a bug. I don't know his name because she wouldn't share that. All I can tell you is he died during the quest. Mother struck a deal with the Grand Duke to claim you, even though he lived in a faraway land. There would be little, if any, contact between the two of you. She thought it was a good idea at the time. The bastard has been black-mailing her for winters, threatening to expose her."

"So, my whole life is a lie to protect Mother's reputation?"

"If the Coven knew the truth, you would have been destroyed at birth. Mother did it to protect you. It's also why she chose to pair you with the necro. She is running out of money to pay off the Duke. If he goes through with his threat, Mother thought you would be safer here with them."

"How do you know all this?"

"Mother shared it with me when I got my stripe. She needed to share the burden of the secret with someone. It's hard to live a lie. By the time I found out, Yeresta already knew for a while. She convinced Mother to tell me."

"So—there it is. I'm the monster child. Why did the four of you even bother coming to my aid?"

"You're our sister. Our Mother's blood flows in you, as it does for us all. I can still remember the sun you got your first wand. You were only six. You ran around the temple tapping everyone's butt and yelling 'you're dead.' Cutest thing I've ever seen. Whether the necros win or lose, I don't want to lose you."

"I guess Yeresta doesn't feel the same way," I said.

"She stayed behind to take care of little Meosa. Mother is falling apart. She's considering killing the Duke. If this all goes sour, Yeresta will have to get Meosa out of the Coven fast. Meosa is too young to understand what's going on. We had to leave her behind for her safety and ours. She would have cried out and given us away. Don't judge your first sister by her absence. This was not an easy decision for any of us. We have all risked everything to be here or to stay behind."

"All this pain—all this mess—it's because of me."

"No. All this mess is because of Mother's love for you. She hid her true feelings, even from you. She wanted people to think you were the useless one. Shielding you from the limelight meant less of a chance of exposure. And then, you had to become a powerful beauty. It's hard to hide a diamond among the salt. When this is over, she'll find a way to reinstate us into the Coven. Mother is better with politics than anyone. She'll make it right."

"Speak of the necro," Thesca said, "here he comes."

"Good evening, ladies," Timikia smiled. "I have some news to share. I don't know how things work in the Coven, but here we have a strict chain of command. Lord Loter, our chief battle commander, has decreed that I will be your commanding officer."

"Like hell you are!" Meca retorted. "I don't answer to any necro, especially a guardian. When the fighting starts, stay out of the way or you'll get burned too. Come on girls, let's find a more private place to talk."

The three eldest arose. Persa and I remained seated.

"I want to stay with Solendra," Persa expressed. "I want to talk with the Prince too."

"Persa!" Meca said. "Fall in line."

"I don't want to. You're always bossing me around. Ever since you got your stripe, you think you're all about it."

"PERSA!"

"Persa," I said, taking her hands, "you should go with the others. I have important things to discuss with the Prince."

"Aww …"

"Persa …"

"All right!"

Persa joined the others and they departed the mess tent.

"I think she has a crush on you."

"That's funny. I have a crush on her sister. She's a sweet, little thing, isn't she? Are you all right? You look troubled."

"It's nothing to concern yourself with," I responded. "What's the latest news?"

"I think Lord Loter just realized a hurricane has blown into the city. I'm sure that's why he put me in charge of your sisters. There are times, I am sure he hates me. Any chance your sisters will follow orders?"

"No."

"Great. Just what I needed. Did their training exclude demon lore too?"

"Yes."

"Then, their lack of compliance with orders puts them at risk. Do they understand that?"

"They don't care. Remember how much I hated you when I first arrived?"

"Hard to forget."

"Meca is worse. The rest of them will take their cues from her."

"Well ... on to other news. Sergeant Kitka wants to discuss formations with you. He wants to be ready in case Lord Loter orders a mounted attack. You have made quite an impression on him, surprisingly, considering his complaints when I first put you in charge."

"Yes," I snickered. "I had to ride circles around him a few times before he buckled down."

"My faith in you is well founded. You're an amazing woman. The Coven must be proud."

"Yeah ... I guess."

"Let me accompany you to the stables. I want to spend time with you. I miss you."

He took my hand and together we proceeded through the camp.

"That's weird," I said.

"What's that, my love?"

"Our footprints in the sand."

"What about them?"

"You don't have any. I see mine, but not yours."

Lifting his boot, there was no impression underneath.

"How do you do that?" I asked.

"Ha ... I don't know. These were Lord Whispa's boots. He always had a high regard for them. Now I'm starting to understand why."

"It's interesting, but what use would that be."

"If I were being tracked, it would be difficult for pursuers to locate me."

"True."

A fireball roared over our heads, its glowing plume stretching across the sky. An explosion rocked one of the housing tents. I heard screams of pain in the distance.

"RETURN FIRE!" yelled a sergeant from atop the wall.

The trebuchets sprang into action, their recoils filling the air with rifling noises. My sisters rushed to my side.

"You, soldier," Timikia ordered, "Take Persa back to the palace. Get her safely to the lower levels."

"I can fight!" Persa complained.

"Persa," I said, "Prince Timikia is right. You're only a level two. It's too dangerous."

Persa looked up to Meca for approval, and Meca gave a single nod. Without any more grousing, Persa went off with the soldier. The five of us ran to the battlements, just as the blackhearts began emerging from the trees.

Chapter #29

Defend the Gate

With a deafening sound, it crunched its way through the trees. The massive structure rolled out like a monster dominating the battlefield. It was the length of a temple and shielded from above by a dark roof.

"That has to be the biggest battering ram I've ever seen," I said.

"Timikia," asked Lady Solendra, "can your gates withstand that?"

"Nothing could withstand that."

Four fireballs roared through the sky targeting our walls. The biggest projectile was headed right for us, so I grabbed Solendra and dove to the floor. Meca waved her wand in a semicircle and formed a dome of solid ice above us. The dome was so thick you could barely see through it. The fireball hit true, cracking the dome and showering us with icy shards, but it held. With another pass of her wand, the dome vanished as quickly as it appeared.

"That's the way we do it in Farondow, necro," Meca said with disgust. "Get up off the ground. You look like a sniveling puppy."

"SWITCH TO FLAMING ARROWS!" Major Deric commanded. "WHEN THE RAM IS IN RANGE, LIGHT IT UP!"

"Flaming arrows aren't going to work," I said to the Sorceri.

"Why do you say that?" Meca asked.

"Look how black that roof is. That's not wood—it's shale. The damn thing is fireproof. We have to stop it before it reaches the gates. Everyone, come on."

"I already told you," Meca said, "I don't take orders from necros."

"Fine, then stay here. When they smash through the gates you and your sisters can take on hundreds, if not thousands, of well-armed blackhearts all by yourself. Good luck with that."

I took Lady Solendra's hand and started for the steps only to be halted in my tracks. Meca had grabbed Solendra's arm, preventing us from leaving. Solendra's eyes darted back and forth between us.

"I'm going with him," she said. "I trust him. If Timikia has a plan, we have to try it. Let me go."

Meca's brow crinkled as she struggled with holding her sister back.

"Sister," Solendra continued, "let—me—go."

Reluctantly, Meca complied. We proceeded down the steps.

"You have a plan, yes?" my Lady asked.

"I'm making it up as I go along. I'll keep you posted."

"AH! Come on, girls," Meca shouted from the wall.

The sisters ran to catch up.

"We're heading for the stables?" Solendra asked.

"I know we don't have a lot of lancers," I said, "but we're going to have to charge the ram. We have to get under that roof and set it ablaze. It's the only way to stop it."

"We have less than sixty horses! It's suicide."

"Maybe, but so is waiting for them to crash the gates. We have to try."

By the time we reached the stables, the slow-moving ram was halfway across the battlefield; its wheels creaked with every turn. Our catapults pounded it with rocks, but they bounced off its protective skin. The towers had switched to standard arrows in an attempt to pick off blackhearts huddled near the exposed edges. As the occasional blackheart would fall, a necromancer would skel it up only to have it crumble into a pile of bones moments later. There he was, standing just to the rear of the machine—the figure in gold. He was releasing every skel as quickly as they were created. Now, I had a plan.

"Mages," I said, "I've seen Lady Solendra become a human flame. Is it safe to assume the rest of you are as incendiary?"

"Of course, Sorceri are the masters of fire."

"If the riders of Surdon can cover you long enough to get close, can you toast that thing?"

"We'll turn it into the biggest candle the demons have ever seen," Meca boasted.

"Great! Hang back and wait for your opening. Captain Solendra, arm your men with shields. I need you to distract their archers. Don't attack, just draw their fire. Buy your sisters as much time as possible."

"And exactly what are you going to be doing?" Tamarica asked in disgust.

"Testing a theory."

"What?"

"These horses are crap," complained Meca.

"Just shut up and ride!" Solendra barked in a rare show of defiance toward her elder sibling.

My helmet shrunk to a perfect fit as I placed it upon my head. After mounting Darkness, I strode to the front of the formation. With the camouflaged gate at my back, I looked into the frightened eyes of the riders. Leadership was the best magic I could conjure up for that occasion.

"You have trained all your lives for this moment. If you fall in this battle, you will arrive on the other side as a hero. Songs will be sung and stories will be told of this moment. You are the Riders of Surdon. Let's teach those bastards to remember that name. FIGHT BRAVE! FIGHT HARD! YAH!"

Screaming to the sky, the lancers poured through the gate. Solendra led them off to draw the archers' fire. The other three Sorceri dashed toward the ram. The General paid no attention to the riders, focusing instead on the sisters. In a feeble attempt, I conjured and launched a bone spear at him. The projectile bounced harmlessly off his armor, but I got his attention.

Using up a good chunk of my mana, I molded my last poison dagger into a metal monster. I squeezed my fists tight, drawing Karoc's spirit into the steel. With minds linked, I mentally gave my golem the order to attack. Karoc rushed in. The General swept his hand to release him, but he charged on unfettered.

Father seemed confused as the metal warrior crashed into him. He tumbled to the ground and rolled, barely avoiding Karoc's next strike. Blasting the golem with emotion, Karoc was sent flying three horse lengths back. Both combatants returned to their feet and struggled on.

A small group of blackhearts left the protection of the ram to attack the sisters. One of my bone spears riffled through the lead blackheart's skull. I skeled up the demon and he attacked the others. A second group emerged, but Thesca and Tamarica pushed them back with a blaze of fireballs. Meca was lining up for her attack run on the ram, when she screamed out in horror.

"PERSA! GO BACK!"

Young Persa was charging the ram on a horse so small it could only be referred to as a pony. A spinning ax hit her in the chest and she flew off her mount. Meca reared her horse around to rescue her baby sister. I pushed Darkness hard to intercept her, until our horses almost collided.

"OUT OF MY WAY, NECRO!"

"No! Finish the mission."

"Out of my way or I'll ice you right off your mount!"

"If you don't destroy the ram, all of this was for nothing. There will be no place to take Persa to heal if we fail. Thesca and I can hold off the General, but you're the one with the big flame. People are dying out here. For the gods' sake, destroy that machine!"

She hesitated for a moment, sneered and drove her horse toward the ram.

"Tamarica," I shouted, "go help Persa. Thesca, we have to hold off the General and buy Meca time."

Karoc was turning green and gagging from one of father's vicious poison attacks. I immediately released him, to spare him the pain of a poisonous death. With his soul free to return to the other side, his metal form melted in a molten puddle.

Thesca charged Timicus with her wand aflame. He erected a massive bone wall to block the searing barrage. Emoting, he blew his own wall back at her. Fragments of bone mashed through her horse's head killing him instantly. Thesca leapt off to avoid being crushed by the falling animal. I reached down and took her hand, swinging her up onto Darkness's back. We charged Timicus. Darkness instinctively attempted to stomp him. He shot a poison blast toward us. In a moment of quick thinking, Thesca burned the poison from the air, causing plumes of dense smoke that hid our adversary. A magic missile ripped through the smog aimed right at my head. My helmet's horns smacked the projectile aside. Blinded by the vapors, I fired bone spears wildly through the dense haze.

Meca started her attack run. Riding circles around the ram, she poured fire beneath its roof. Screams of agony filled the air as blackhearts stumbled out of the blaze, their skin melting off their bodies. The ram exploded into a massive inferno. With the task completed, I gave the order to fall back.

Tamarica took an arrow to the shoulder as she lifted Persa's motionless body onto her horse. With a grimace, she heroically struggled on.

Father raised his fist and cried out in a demon tongue. Six massive demon-dogs tore out of the forest. They were bigger than horses with teeth to match.